OVER EVERY HURDLE

ALSO BY BARBARA HINSKE

Available at Amazon in Print, Audio, and for Kindle

The Rosemont Series

Coming to Rosemont

Weaving the Strands

Uncovering Secrets

Drawing Close

Bringing Them Home

Shelving Doubts

Restoring What Was Lost

No Matter How Far

When Dreams There Be

Novellas

The Night Train

The Christmas Club (adapted

for The Hallmark Channel, 2019)

Paws & Pastries

Sweets & Treats

Snowflakes, Cupcakes & Kittens (coming 2023)

Workout Wishes & Valentine Kisses

Wishes of Home

Novels in the Guiding Emily Series

Guiding Emily

The Unexpected Path

Over Every Hurdle

Down the Aisle

Novels in the "Who's There?!" Collection

Deadly Parcel

Final Circuit

CONNECT WITH BARBARA HINSKE ONLINE

Sign up for her newsletter at **BarbaraHinske.com**
Goodreads.com/BarbaraHinske
Facebook.com/BHinske
Instagram/barbarahinskeauthor
TikTok.com/BarbaraHinske
Pinterest.com/BarbaraHinske
Twitter.com/BarbaraHinske
Search for **Barbara Hinske on YouTube**
bhinske@gmail.com

OVER EVERY HURDLE

BOOK THREE OF THE GUIDING EMILY SERIES

BARBARA HINSKE

CASA DEL NORTHERN PUBLISHING

Copyright © 2022 Barbara Hinske.

Cover by Elizabeth Mackey, Copyright © 2022

ISBN: 978-1-7349249-8-5

Library of Congress Control Number: 2022913354

Casa del Northern Publishing

Phoenix, Arizona

With profound gratitude to Dr. David J. Anderson, Dr. Paul M. Petelin, Jr., and Dr. James L. Plotnik for restoring my vision. Thank you will never be enough.

CHAPTER 1

$\mathcal{E}$ mily Main lifted a handful of her heavy auburn hair with one hand and fanned the damp nape of her neck with the other. "What do you think? Does the buffet look pretty? I want everything to be perfect. It needs to be elegant and classy for Gina."

Martha Main put her arm around her daughter's shoulders and gave them a squeeze. "It's absolutely gorgeous. The tea sandwiches you girls made this morning look fantastic. So dainty."

"I cut off all the crusts," Zoe chimed in, proud of her contribution. The fourth grader had recently become Emily's ward when her grandmother had died.

"You did a very precise job of it," Martha told the girl, whom she loved like a granddaughter. She turned to Emily, "The pastries you got from the bakery on the corner are stunning. They're little works of art."

"Thank you for making the scones, Mom. Yours are better than any I've had in a tearoom."

"I'm delighted I could contribute something to Gina's bridal shower," Martha replied. "I'm so happy she's marrying such a nice man. And I'm overjoyed that the two of you have rekindled your friendship."

Emily inhaled deeply. The rift between her and her life-long best friend had been a painful chapter in her life. One she was thankful was finally over. "Did you put the flowers on the end table?" she asked Zoe.

"Yep. They're next to the sign that says 'Gifts.' Every-thing's set up like the map we made. Do you want me to lead you around the room so you can check everything?"

Emily shook her head. "That's not necessary. If you say it's all right, then it is. You're very reliable, Zoe—way more dependable than I was at your age." She wished she could see Zoe's reaction to her words, but Zoe's quick intake of breath told Emily that Zoe appreciated the compliment.

"How long before people start arriving?" Emily asked.

Martha consulted her watch. "Any minute now. Are you still expecting seven, including Gina?"

"Yes. It's a family shower. I hope Gina isn't disappointed. I didn't think I could manage—"

"Gina's thrilled you're doing this for her. I talked to her mother yesterday. Gina will have time to relax and talk to everyone. Her mother told me she's really looking forward to this afternoon."

Emily nodded. "Good. And Garth is in his bed? He's not working as my guide dog during the shower."

"He's stretched out and sound asleep," Zoe said. "Sabrina's cuddled up next to him."

"Okay. We don't want them getting under anyone's feet. It's your job to make sure Sabrina stays out of the way, Zoe."

"I know," Zoe said, a hint of rebuke in her voice.

Martha rubbed the girl's back in a circular motion. "It's always a bit nerve-wracking for the host right before a party starts. You keep going over the details in your mind to make sure you haven't forgotten anything."

"Let's put hot water into the teapots to warm them," Emily said. "There should be ten of them. Everyone can select their own tea from the box. We have twenty different varieties. It came in handy that you're such a big tea drinker, Mom."

Martha moved to the kitchen island and began filling the individual teapots with hot water from the large electric urn. "I had so much fun shopping for the teas for this shower. I also bought enough new kinds to try at home that I won't run out for at least a year."

"Thank you for letting me borrow teapots from your collection," Emily said.

"They're all so pretty," Zoe chimed in.

"I'm happy that they're getting pressed into service," Martha said. "I love them, but I rarely use them. I just plop a tea bag into a mug at home."

"If I drank tea every day and had a teapot, I'd use it," Zoe said.

"Quite right. Is one of these your favorite?" Martha asked.

Zoe walked to the kitchen island and stood, surveying the

ten teapots lined up in two rows. "It's a tie between the one with yellow daisies that are sort of raised up on the sides and the one that's a shiny bright blue."

"You've got a good eye," Martha said. "The one with the daisies is handmade. My husband got it for me in Sausalito for our first anniversary. It's my favorite. The other one is Fiestaware."

"I'll tell you what—let's put both of these aside so that Zoe can have the blue one for her teapot and you can have the one Dad gave you for yours, Mom."

"Can we?" Zoe asked.

"Of course," Emily said as the buzzer from the lobby sounded. She made her way to the door and pressed the button to open the lobby door. "I think our first guests are here. Go do that quickly, Zoe. It's showtime!"

GINA ROBERTS and her mother swept into Emily's apartment. "Are we the first to arrive?" Gina asked as she drew Emily into a hug. "It's poor form for the bride to be late."

"Mom and Zoe are here, of course," Emily said. "But no one else."

"Good. We had a heck of a time finding a parking spot. Drove around the block twice." Hilary Roberts, Gina's mother, walked up to Emily and took both of her hands in hers. "Hello, dear girl. I…" her voice broke. "This is the first time I've seen you since…" She drew in a deep breath.

"Since I lost my eyesight," Emily finished her sentence for her. "I know. You've been on your retirement round-the-world tour. How was it?"

Hilary cleared her throat. "It was wonderful—mostly. We saw everything on our bucket list and decided on a few places we'd like to go back to, but being away for over a year was too much for me. If it hadn't been for Charles, I would have bolted for home months ahead of schedule."

"I was proud of you for stepping out of your comfort zone and going," Emily said. "I'd love to hear more about your favorite experiences during tea."

"I'll sit with you this afternoon and do just that." Hilary stepped back, holding Emily at arm's length. "You look terrific, Em. You've always been beautiful, and you're still full of the self-confidence, poise, and presence you've always had." They remained silent. "I'm so glad."

"Thank you," Emily said quietly. "The past couple of years have been rough, but Mom's been a rock star this whole time and I've been blessed with the most supportive co-workers you could ever hope for—not to mention Gina. The training I've received from the Foundation for the Blind has allowed me to resume my independent life, and having Garth at my side," she gestured to where her guide dog lay on his bed in a corner of the room, "is... well... everything."

"Gina told me you have a remarkable guide dog," Hilary said. "There are two dogs over there."

"The schnauzer is mine," Zoe said. "She's not trained to be a guide dog, but she's really smart—just like Garth."

"You must be Zoe," Hilary said, turning to the girl. She

5

extended her hand; Zoe took it and they shook. "I'm Gina's mom. You can call me Hilary. My daughter thinks the world of you. She says you've been extremely helpful to Emily—and that you've been through a lot, too."

Zoe sidled over to Emily.

"I was so sorry to hear about your grandmother. I knew Irene and liked her very much."

Zoe swallowed hard, and Emily put her arm around the little girl's shoulders.

"That's a very pretty dress you're wearing, Zoe," Gina broke in. "The yellow is beautiful with your dark hair and eyes. Vibrant. It suits you."

Martha caught Zoe's eye and winked at her.

Zoe flushed. "I love this color."

The buzzer sounded again, and Emily moved toward the sound. She pressed the button to open the lobby door. "We're going to have tea as soon as everyone arrives. Then we'll open gifts."

"Did you receive mine?" Hilary asked. "I had the store send it here."

Emily nodded. "It's in my bedroom. Zoe—can you get the wrapped package that's sitting on top of the dresser and put it on the gifts table?"

Zoe took off to retrieve Hilary's gift as Emily buzzed in another guest and opened her door.

"Emily," called a vaguely familiar voice. "I'm Craig's aunt. We met at the engagement party I threw for Craig and Gina."

"Yes—I remember. It was a..." She paused, searching for the right words. She'd spent the entire party secluded in the

library of the palatial Georgian home, avoiding the bois-
terous party while getting to know Craig's twin brother,
Grant Johnson. Not only getting to know him, but becoming
romantically interested in him.

"Grant can't stop talking about you," the woman behind
Grant's aunt chimed in. "Sylvia Johnson," said the woman,
taking Emily's hand in hers. "I'm Craig and Grant's mother.
I'm pleased to meet you. Thank you so much for inviting
me."

Emily and Sylvia shook hands warmly. Emily could feel a
flush rise up from the open neckline of her floral-patterned
dress. She and Grant had spoken on the phone almost every
night since they'd met but had only found time to see each
other twice—once for dinner and another time for a
midweek cup of coffee. His busy schedule as an architect and
widowed father, together with her demanding job and new
responsibilities with Zoe, allowed scant time for their
budding relationship. She was pleased that he'd spoken
about her to his mother.

"Please... come in," Emily said, stepping aside.

"I want to introduce you to someone else," Sylvia said. "I
hope you don't mind that we brought her along. Meet
Diedre—Grant's daughter."

"Hi Diedre! Your dad's told me so much about you."
Emily spoke into the space in front of her. "I'm glad you
decided to come, after all."

"I talked her into it," Gina said. "I told her that there'd be
another girl here her age, so it would be fun for her. I figured
you'd have more than enough food."

"Of course," Emily said. "As a matter of fact, I think both you and Zoe are new fourth graders at Hillside Elementary. I don't believe you're in the same class, but maybe you've seen each other."

Diedre shrugged and stared at the floor.

Sylvia bent over and spoke softly into Diedre's ear. "Emily is like your other grandfather. She can't see, so you have to talk to her."

The buzzer sounded again.

"That'll be my three cousins," Gina said. "They were driving into San Francisco together. We're all here! Let's get this party started."

CHAPTER 2

$\mathscr{I}$ cracked one eye open and lifted my head a quarter inch from my bed. The buzzer was sounding intermittently and with each buzz, Emily was welcoming more females into our apartment.

Their excited chatter filled the room with an expectant energy. Dressed in their finery, they confirmed the growing suspicion I'd had all morning as Emily, Zoe, and Martha had raced around the apartment, setting out food, rearranging furniture, and plumping pillows. We were having a party. I thought I remembered Emily calling it a bridal shower.

My harness was hanging from its usual hook by the door, so I knew I wasn't working the party. Emily had put me in my bed and told me to "stay." Fine by me. An afternoon nap was always welcome and something I excelled at.

Zoe had placed Sabrina on the bed with me. I'd grown to love my pal Sabrina. I even thought of her as my best friend

—after Emily, of course. But Sabrina didn't have the discipline I had. She wouldn't do as she'd been told. It was only a matter of time before she would get up and start zooming around the room in that miniature schnauzer way of hers, annoying everyone.

I noticed a young girl enter the room. She looked to be the same size as Zoe. Dogs are highly empathic creatures, with guide dogs being at the top of the class in this regard. I could tell right away that this girl was as anxious as she was insecure.

I pushed myself up into a half-sitting position and observed the scene in front of me. I wasn't able to determine what had gotten her down but I was certain that I'd be able to help her.

I might have to disobey Emily and break my "stay." I wouldn't do it lightly. I continued to scrutinize the actions of the humans in the room.

If I had the opportunity to help this girl, I'd be ready to leap into action.

CHAPTER 3

*E*mily shut the door and rested her back against it. "Welcome, everyone," she said, raising her voice slightly to be heard above the chorus of greetings. "Zoe and I are so glad you could come to our shower for Gina. Zoe—can you say 'hi' to everyone?"

"Hi," came the tentative reply.

"Zoe will take your cards and packages and put them on the gifts table. I thought we should go around the room to introduce ourselves with our name and how we know Gina. Then we'll have tea and open presents. Zoe—would you like to start?"

The room grew quiet.

"I'm Zoe," the girl said softly and paused.

"Zoe's my newest best friend," Gina supplied, going to stand next to her.

Martha took the next turn and soon everyone was on a first-name basis.

Emily took charge again. "We've got five different tea sandwiches—all expertly prepared by Zoe; the best scones on the West coast, care of Martha; and desserts that are almost too pretty to eat from the bakery on the corner."

A murmur of approval floated around the room as the guests eyed the buffet set up on the kitchen island.

"Everyone gets their own individual teapot. Pick your favorite one and select a tea from the box on the counter. We've warmed the pots. Martha will fill it for you from the electric urn that contains hot water. Take your tea and plates into the living room. I've got tea cups arranged in a basket on the coffee table, together with cream and sugar for those who would like them."

Emily turned in the direction of the kitchen. "Gina— you're the guest of honor. You go first."

"Will do," Gina replied, "after I finish taking pictures of everything for my social media." She turned back to address Emily. "It looks absolutely stunning, Em. Like it was styled for a lifestyle magazine."

"That's all Zoe's doing," Emily replied. "She's got an artistic eye."

"Nicely done, Zoe!" Gina said.

"Martha helped me," Zoe said.

"I didn't change anything," Martha said. "You laid it all out. After Gina, why don't we let Diedre and you go next? You've met at school, haven't you?"

Zoe nodded as Hilary drew Diedre forward.

"We've seen each other," Diedre mumbled.

"Now you two can get to know each other," Hilary said.

"The teapots are here." Zoe pointed to the eight vessels lined up on the island.

"That one on the counter—behind you—is the same blue as your dress, Diedre," Hilary exclaimed, pointing to the Fiestaware teapot that Martha had set aside for Zoe. "I know it's your favorite color. Would you like to choose it?"

Zoe's head whipped around. She locked eyes with Martha. Martha shook her head imperceptibly.

"That'd be great," Diedre said.

"Select your tea from the box," Hilary said.

Zoe opened her mouth to speak and Martha put her hand on Zoe's shoulder, bringing her lips close to Zoe's ear. "She's the guest—let her have the blue pot. I'm going to leave it here so we can use it for tea whenever I come to visit. Would you like that?"

Zoe nodded her head.

"Why don't you sit with Diedre? It'll be nice for you to have a new friend at school."

"I don't need a new friend at school," Zoe muttered. "I'm fine."

Everyone served themselves and congregated in the living room. Zoe did as Martha had suggested and perched on the sofa next to Diedre. The foggy morning had given way to a cloudless afternoon and sunshine slanted through the tall windows, creating swaths of warm light on the carpeted floor. The room was soon filled with the sound of silver cutlery scraping china plates, moans of appreciation over the delicious food, and animated conversation punctuated by laughter.

Zoe and Diedre sat next to each other, their plates balanced awkwardly on their knees. The girls snuck surreptitious glances at each other but remained silent.

Sabrina, who had obediently remained in the dog bed with Garth, finally abandoned her post. She approached the group slowly, snuffling her nose along the floor, hoping to find a dropped morsel. When she reached Zoe, Sabrina hopped onto the sofa between the girls.

Zoe clutched her plate, but Diedre didn't react as quickly. Sabrina's intrusion upended Diedre's plate against the front of her beautiful blue dress. A scone, lathered with Devonshire cream, slipped down the bodice and deposited itself in Diedre's lap.

Diedre jerked back in her seat, a look of horror on her face.

"Stupid dog," she muttered as she grabbed her napkin and began swiping at the mess on the front of her dress.

"Sabrina's not stupid," Zoe retorted. "She's just a dog. It was an accident."

Tears pooled in Diedre's eyes and dripped onto the growing stain.

"Oh, my gosh. Look at you!" Sylvia set her teacup on the coffee table. "What a mess." She took the napkin from Diedre. "You're just making it worse. Come with me." Sylvia took her granddaughter's hand and pulled her to her feet. "We'll go into the kitchen and get you cleaned up in no time."

She looked into Diedre's face, now streaming with tears. "Don't cry, darling. This dress is washable. It'll all be fine."

Diedre stepped around the coffee table to go with her grandmother.

"I'm sorry. Sabrina and I are so sorry," Zoe said to Diedre's retreating back in a voice so soft that no one heard.

CHAPTER 4

W ell—that didn't go well.

I should have forced myself to stay awake. I'd only intended to take a catnap, which is a stupid name for a short nap as far as I'm concerned. Cats can out-sleep the best of us.

I just knew that Sabrina didn't have the necessary self-control to remain in our bed as ordered. I figured she'd go hunting for crumbs. I'd sized this group up from the get-go and knew that they weren't sloppy eaters. None of these ladies would drop food on the floor. That's why I'd opted for a nap.

I'd woken with a start when the other little girl and a woman entered the kitchen. One look at the girl's dress, together with the talking-to that Sabrina was getting from Zoe, and I guessed what had happened.

I also knew that the other girl's sense of sadness had

deepened—and there was now a definite sense of wariness between Zoe and this girl.

Oh, boy. I didn't know what I could do about this. Some things are above my pay grade. I'd have to think carefully before I took any sort of action.

CHAPTER 5

"*H*i Stephanie—and Biscuit," Emily said.

"I was hoping we'd run into the two of you out here," Stephanie said to her close friend. They'd met and formed an instant bond when they were both students at the Foundation for the Blind.

Biscuit led her handler to the spot of grass behind their apartment building reserved for dogs. Garth had just finished and made way for his fellow guide dog to access the grass.

"How was your shower? Zoe talked about nothing else when we walked back and forth to school last week. She was so excited."

"It was a lot of fun. Gina and Craig's family get along really well. Everyone raved about the food, which Zoe and my mom deserve all the credit for. I was nervous about throwing her a shower, but now that it's over, I'm so glad I did."

"Craig and Grant are brothers, aren't they?"

"Twins."

"So you met your boyfriend's mom. How did you like her?"

"She's really very nice."

"Does she know that you're dating her son?"

"She said that Grant can't stop talking about me." Emily's pleasure in this fact rang through in her voice.

"I'm not surprised. Who wouldn't love you, Em?"

"I also met Grant's daughter. Diedre."

"The one that goes to Hillside?"

"Yep. She's in fourth grade, like Zoe, but they're not in the same class."

"I don't know the fourth graders," Stephanie replied, "since this is my first year teaching third grade. Did she and Zoe have a good time getting to know each other?"

Emily's shoulders drooped, and she turned her face to the ground. "I don't know. We weren't expecting her, so when her grandmother brought her to the shower, I was really pleased. Zoe's never had a wide circle of friends and I thought this might be nice for her." Emily paused.

"And?"

"I can't get anything more out of Zoe than that Diedre's 'okay.' She has no enthusiasm in her voice and she shuts down the minute I want to talk."

Stephanie chuckled.

"What's funny?"

"If I had a nickel for every parent who's said that about their child..."

"So this is normal?"

"Perfectly."

They stood together in silence as Biscuit circled and found her spot.

"I understand your concern about Zoe being... isolated. She's a very gifted student—way ahead of her grade level in all subjects, yet she's still emotionally and developmentally a fourth grader."

"I know she's brilliant, but I want her to be a child, too. She needs to have all the pleasures of childhood—including having a best friend."

"I agree. These advanced kids can be a challenge. What did you think of Diedre? Was she nice?"

"Yes—at least I think she was. I didn't spend much time with her. Diedre got upset when Sabrina jumped on the sofa and knocked her plate into her dress. She started crying. I understand it made a mess, but it was no big deal. Her grandmother helped her clean it up."

"Hmmm..." Stephanie faced Emily. "Relationships between these pre-adolescent girls are fraught with misunderstandings and emotion. Let me try to get Zoe to talk to me about it when we walk to school together in the morning."

"Would you? I'd like to know what's troubling her. If she and Diedre can't get along, then maybe I shouldn't be dating Grant. What would be the point?"

"Hang on," Stephanie said quickly. "You really like Grant

and, from what you say, he's a great guy. Don't throw that away over some imagined tiff between fourth-grade girls. I'll do some digging and let you know."

"You're the best, Stephanie. Please don't let on that I put you up to this."

"No worries on that score. Subtlety is my middle name. I'll call you if I get any news to share."

"COME ON," Emily said, turning to address the girl who was dawdling as she made her way along the corridor to Stephanie's studio apartment. Emily barely needed her cane as she took the final few steps to the apartment where she had lived until a few weeks ago. Soon after Zoe's grandmother had died and Emily had become Zoe's legal guardian, they'd moved downstairs to a spacious three-bedroom unit in the well-appointed old building.

At the same time, Stephanie had been searching—without success—for lodging near Hillside Elementary, where she'd just secured a position as a third-grade teacher. Allowing Stephanie to take over Emily's lease had been the perfect solution. That Zoe could walk back and forth to school with Stephanie and Biscuit, and stay with Stephanie until Emily got home from work, solved a myriad of issues.

Emily opened her arms wide, and Zoe stepped into them. "What's got your goat this morning?"

"Nothing."

"Are you feeling okay?" Emily pressed her palm against Zoe's forehead. "You don't have a fever."

"I'm fine," Zoe said without conviction.

"Are you happy at your school, honey?"

Zoe shrugged. "Sure."

"Everyone gets down in the dumps from time to time. Making a start on your day is usually all it takes to brush the blues away." Emily hugged Zoe to her as the door opened.

Stephanie and Biscuit stood in the doorway.

"Hi," Zoe said quickly. "We're to the right of the door."

"We were just coming to get you," Stephanie said. "We don't want to be late."

"Have a good day, you two," Emily said. "Don't forget to take Sabrina out as soon as you get home."

"I won't," Zoe said.

"Zoe always remembers what she needs to do," Stephanie said as she and Biscuit led the way to the elevator. "And she starts her homework without my having to say a word to her."

"She's a very responsible person," Emily said, swiveling to Zoe. "I guess I remind you of things out of habit. Sorry."

"That's okay," Zoe said. "Grandma did it all the time, too."

"It's a parental thing," Stephanie chimed in.

"I should be home on time tonight," Emily said. "I'm going in early so I can review a memo Dhruv sent me over the weekend. When he gets in this morning, I want to discuss it with him."

"He texted me an hour ago," Stephanie chuckled. "He's already at the office."

"Really? What's got him so fired up?"

"He never talks about his work in any detail," Stephanie replied. "Not that I would understand it, anyway, but he said it has something to do with cybersecurity."

"Holy cow," Emily said. "That's an enormous concern these days, but it's not what our unit works on. I can't wait to read what he's written."

The elevator doors opened.

"See you tonight," Emily said. "I'm going to get Garth, and we'll be on our way."

"See you, Em," Zoe said as she followed Stephanie and Biscuit out of the building and onto the sidewalk.

"You had a busy weekend, what with the shower and all," Stephanie said. "Emily said that you did a beautiful job with the tea sandwiches and were a wonderful help. She said she couldn't have done it without you."

They walked together, the traffic noise of the busy city mingling with the occasional bird call.

"Did you have fun at the shower?" Stephanie asked.

"I guess."

"Tell me about it."

"We had tea and Gina opened her presents. Then we played games."

"That sounds nice."

They continued walking in silence, and Stephanie was about to ask another question when Zoe spoke.

"I spoiled the tea part."

"What are you talking about? What happened?"

"There was a girl from my grade there—Diedre. She's one

of the 'popular' girls. I didn't make Sabrina stay out of the way, and when she jumped on the sofa, Sabrina knocked Diedre's plate into the front of her dress. It was a big mess and Diedre cried."

"That sounds like an accident," Stephanie said. "That wasn't your fault."

"Except it was. I saw Sabrina sneaking around, looking for food dropped on the floor. I knew I should have put her back on the bed with Garth. If I'd done that, it wouldn't have happened."

"I'm sure it's not as bad as you think. Diedre will have forgotten all about it by now."

"You think so?"

"I do, but what are you afraid of?"

"That she'll tell the other cool kids that I messed up. They'll make fun of me." Zoe's breathing came rapidly. "Those kids already don't like me."

"Why do you say that?"

"I sit at lunch with a couple of the boys. We work together in an advanced math group and we're all interested in science." Zoe's next statement was factual and not boastful. "We're the smartest kids in the school."

"Ah… so you assume they don't like you because you're smart?"

"The boys have been at this school since kindergarten and they say they're mean girls—those girls make fun of them and call them nerds and dorks."

"But you'd like to have a girlfriend?"

"Yes. Like you and Emily. Or Em and Gina. Is that so horrible?"

"Of course not! It's perfectly natural." Stephanie waited, giving Zoe a chance to expound. When Zoe remained quiet, Stephanie continued. "In my experience, when people don't like each other, it's because they don't really know each other. They're making unfounded assumptions based upon misunderstandings."

"So, what do I do about it?"

"Give them the benefit of the doubt. Don't jump to conclusions. Be nice to them. Smile and say 'hi.' " Her voice held the hint of a smile. "Use the scientific method. Wait and observe what happens."

"I guess I can try it."

"Good. Let me know how it goes, okay? I'm here for you, any time."

They approached the iron gates that marked the pedestrian entrance to Hillside Elementary.

"We're here, aren't we?" Stephanie asked.

"We just walked through the gates. How can you tell?"

"Biscuit pulls on her harness a bit differently. I know we're about to peel off to the left to our classroom."

"She's so smart!"

"That she is. Chin up, Zoe. Everything will be fine."

CHAPTER 6

*E*mily stepped off the elevator on the floor that housed her office and that of her team of elite programmers. It was an hour before the start of her workday. She gave Garth the command to take her to the left.

"Good morning, Dhruv," Emily said before they'd taken another handful of steps toward her office.

"Hey, Emily," Dhruv replied. He glanced at Garth, who kept his eyes on the path in front of him, but whose tail swished from side to side with extra energy. "He gave me away, didn't he?"

Emily laughed. "He sure did. Next to me and Zoe, I think you're his favorite human."

"I sent you a memo over the weekend," Dhruv began.

"I know. I peeked at my inbox last night and Stephanie mentioned that you'd come in early this morning to talk to me about it first thing."

"Will you let me know when you've read it?"

"I already have. We took a rideshare this morning and I listened to the screen reader on my headphones on the way." Emily addressed Garth. "Find my office."

Dhruv fell in step next to her and Garth. "What do you think?"

"You've done a thorough job of laying out the threat to the company from a cyberattack and have outlined a comprehensive program to combat and respond to such an attack."

Garth led them through an open doorway. Emily took three steps forward to her desk. She deposited her purse in the deep bottom drawer and placed her laptop on the desk. She sat in her chair and Garth settled under the desk, at her feet.

Dhruv hovered in the doorway.

She continued, "Do you think a computer program can be created with all the functionality you describe?"

"I know it can," said the most brilliant programmer she'd ever worked with. "I know what programming language I'd use, and I came in early this morning to work on a chart of how the program would work."

"That's admirable, Dhruv. I love how you think outside the box and aren't afraid to tackle any problem."

"Cyberattacks are our biggest threat," he stated. "I can't stop thinking about them."

"... but the company has an entire team devoted to cyber-security."

"The people working in cybersecurity here aren't up to

the task. You've heard the same rumors I have: they're floundering."

Emily cleared her throat. "Even so, we can't just take this on. Our workload is through the roof, as it is."

"We could hire lower-level programmers to handle what we're doing now. We could supervise them. You, Rhonda, Mike and I can write the program in my memo."

Emily pursed her lips. She was aware of upper management's dissatisfaction with the progress being made to combat cybersecurity, but that team wasn't even in the same division of the company as her team. You had to go up four rungs of the corporate ladder to get to the person to whom both her team and the cybersecurity team reported. Emily had never talked to the person three rungs up, let alone four.

"We need to do this, Emily." Dhruv stated the matter as an obvious certainty. "Tell them."

"It's not that simple, Dhruv."

"Don't you think my plan will work?"

"I'd have to look into it more deeply... but yes, I think it would."

"Don't you think we can do it?"

"Of course I think we could do it." Emily forced herself not to smile. Dhruv always boiled any problem down to its most basic elements. His singular laser focus sometimes proved difficult in everyday life, but it was a tremendous benefit in his profession. "Tasks are assigned around here based on company politics as often as they are on the skill sets of the teams involved."

"That's stupid."

"I agree with you, but it doesn't change reality."

"You're very good at company politics. Mike says so all the time."

"Thank you, but what you're suggesting involves politics way above my level."

"I think you can do it."

Emily sighed heavily. Dhruv was on a mission and there would be no diverting him. When Emily had been in a deep depression after losing her eyesight, Dhruv's tenacity had saved her. She'd confined herself to her room and refused to enroll in the training programs at the Foundation for the Blind that ultimately allowed her to reclaim her independent life. Dhruv had driven the hour to Martha's house every evening for weeks until he and the other members of her team had convinced her she needed to come out of her cave and accept help. She would always be profoundly grateful to this man with the giant brain and the even bigger heart.

"Let me think about it," Emily said.

"Good. You'll figure it out."

"It won't be easy. I may not be successful."

"You will be."

"It might take months. We have to remain focused on our current responsibilities."

"We will. I'm only working on this in my spare time."

Emily sighed in exasperation. "You're not supposed to be working on things on your own time!"

"I can't stop my brain…" His words trailed off, and she knew he was walking away, secure in the belief she would make this happen.

29

Emily opened a desk drawer and withdrew the water bowl that she kept in her office for Garth. She sunk into her desk chair, deep in thought. Dhruv's idea might be exactly what the company needed. She agreed with his assessment—the four of them could handle most of the work and she felt certain the company would allow her to hire additional programmers to help.

She got slowly to her feet. She was overdue for a promotion. The company had been extremely accommodating to her while she'd been on family medical leave after the accident on her honeymoon had caused her retinas to detach, plunging her into blindness. They'd gone above and beyond in providing her with all the assistive technology she'd needed to do her job. With the support of her team, she'd regained her confidence in her abilities. Emily had been ready for a promotion when she'd lost her sight—it was time, now, to ask to move to the next level. Pitching this cybersecurity program to the higher-ups might be her ticket to achieving this goal.

Emily grasped Garth's harness. "Let's get you some water. I need to devise a way to make Dhruv's plan a reality."

CHAPTER 7

$\mathcal{I}$ knew the minute I stepped off the elevator that something was up. Dhruv has always had a tendency to be intense, but the way he held his shoulders—sort of up around his ears—told me he was worked up about something.

Emily didn't seem to mind, however. When we went into her office, she seemed a bit cautious. But as they talked, I could hear the undercurrent of excitement in her voice. If whatever Dhruv wanted to do made Emily sound this way—well—I was all for it.

As their conversation went on, I was worried that we were veering too far away from our normal routine. I needn't have worried. Emily pulled out my water bowl and got me settled in for a morning of office work just as soon as Dhruv walked away.

My only lingering complaint was that Dhruv hadn't

asked to give me one of the treats he always had in his pocket for me. The ones that Emily always said yes to.

I stretched out under Emily's desk. The familiar click as her fingers flew across her keyboard was making my eyes heavy. I put my head on my paws.

The day was still young. Dhruv would be back. I was sure he'd remember my treat next time.

CHAPTER 8

"Are you sure you're not moving out, instead of going to a sleepover birthday party?" Grant asked his daughter.

"Daaaad." Diedre drew out the word. "I can't sleep without my own pillow. We're going swimming—there's an indoor pool in her building—so I need my bathing suit. And we're going to make soap, so that could be messy. I'll need clean clothes after that. Plus an outfit for tomorrow." She inserted her arms through the straps of one of the two backpacks on the floor by the garage door and hoisted it onto her back. "The only other thing we have to take is her gift."

"Already in the car." Grant opened the door and grabbed her other backpack. "Is Zoe going to the party too?"

Diedre's back stiffened at the sound of Zoe's name. "NO."

"Why did you say it like that?" Grant buckled his seat belt and met Diedre's eyes in the rearview mirror.

"She's not friends with us."

"Okay."

"She's not in the same class as us. We don't hang out with her."

He started the car. "You said you had a good time at the shower—and she was there. I thought you might become friends, since you're both new at the school."

Diedre turned her face to the window. "It doesn't work like that."

"I don't understand, honey. You've always been friends with everyone. What's going on?"

"Zoe's different. She doesn't like me."

"Why do you say that? You're not still upset that her dog knocked your plate onto your dress? That was an accident."

"I know, Dad! It's not that."

"Then what is it?"

"She's a brainiac, Dad. She thinks I'm stupid."

"Oh, come on. You don't really believe that."

Diedre remained silent as they drove.

"You're extremely smart," Grant said. "We both know that. You're dyslexic and that poses challenges, but you overcome them brilliantly."

"Other people don't know that about me, Dad. I take longer to do stuff than most people, and they assume I'm dumb."

"That's not true. And why would Zoe think that, anyway?"

"Because we played two games at the shower. One was a word search and the other had us guess the number of jelly beans in a jar." Diedre sighed heavily. "Zoe won them both, and she finished way before time was up."

"No one thinks you're dumb because you didn't win a bridal shower game. By that logic, everyone else there is dumb because they didn't win." He caught her eyes in the rearview mirror again and raised his eyebrows at her.

"She looked at my paper, Dad. On the word search. She saw I hadn't even gotten one when she'd already finished. She rolled her eyes and I know what she was thinking."

Grant pulled to the curb in front of a swanky-looking modern condominium tower. "You're imagining things, Diedre. I'm sure Zoe thought nothing of it." He got out of the car and retrieved her pillow and both backpacks.

Diedre picked up her gift and followed him through the massive glass doors into the building's lobby. They checked in with the attendant, who pointed to the elevator bank. Diedre pushed the elevator button for her friend's floor.

"I'll be back to pick you up tomorrow morning at eleven," Grant said. "Be sure to stay up all night."

"You know I can't do that." Diedre smiled. "What are you doing tonight?"

They got into the elevator.

"I'm going out to dinner."

Diedre looked up at him. "With Grandma and Grandpa?"

Grant shook his head. "Emily Main."

Diedre stepped back. "Why her?"

"She's the woman I met at your Uncle Craig's engagement party. I told you about her—and that we've gotten together a couple of times."

"I didn't know she was Zoe's..."

The elevator stopped, and the door opened onto a hallway humming with activity. Two other parents and party-goers were gathered in front of the second doorway on the right, waiting for the door to be opened. The girls were pointing to the colorful balloon arch surrounding the door as their parents labored under their burden of back-packs, pillows, and gifts.

The other elevator arrived on the floor just after the one that had carried Grant and Diedre. Three other girls and their similarly laden parents emerged.

The front door opened, and the birthday girl emerged, hugging her friends as they surrounded her.

Grant followed them all inside and deposited Diedre's things with the growing pile of like items along one wall in the living room. He caught Diedre's eye in the gaggle of girls and raised a hand to wave goodbye. He mouthed the words, "Have fun."

With her eyes narrow and her expression serious, Diedre nodded.

Grant weaved his way to the door through additional arriving guests and retraced his steps to his car. Females were certainly mysterious creatures, he thought to himself as he replayed his conversation with Diedre in his mind. For the life of him, he couldn't see how she could have concluded that Zoe didn't like her. He pursed his lips. If he and Emily were to have a future, Diedre and Zoe would have to get along. First, though, he'd have to get to know Emily Main better. The thought brought a smile to his face. He was looking forward to doing that in a few hours.

"You're sure you don't mind having Zoe for a few hours?" Emily said quietly to Stephanie so that her ward wouldn't overhear. "It is Saturday night. Don't you and Dhruv go out?"

"Once in a while, but we're both homebodies and really prefer to stay in. We go out to eat during the week, but Dhruv loves to cook on the weekend. We usually watch a movie or play Scrabble after dinner."

"Zoe loves to do both."

"I know." Stephanie's voice was full of warmth. "Dhruv likes to play with her. He says she gives him a run for his money."

Emily chuckled. "I'll bet she does. She's been looking forward to this all week. I'm glad that I can leave her without feeling guilty."

"You go out with that new man of yours and have a great time," Stephanie replied.

"I wouldn't describe him as 'that new man of mine.'"

"Yet," Stephanie quickly supplied. "Give it time. My fingers are crossed."

"Thank you. It would be nice to have someone special in my life. You and Dhruv are doing great. Are things getting serious?"

"We're taking it slowly," Stephanie said, "but I'd say 'yes' to that. We're committed to each other and seeing where this leads."

"I'm so happy for you." Emily squeezed Stephanie's hand. "I'd better get back upstairs to get Garth. Grant should be here any minute."

"Have fun, Em."

"Thanks. We won't be late." Emily raised her chin. "Bye, Zoe. I'll be back before you know it."

Zoe came to stand by Emily. "By eight, do you think?"

"I think we'll be a bit later than that." Emily chuckled.

"What time, then?" Zoe whined.

"I should think I'll be home by ten. Does that work for you?"

Zoe stared at the floor and remained silent.

"Zoe? What is it? You'll get to stay up past ten. You love that."

"Okay." Zoe's shoulder shook with her heavy sigh. "See you by ten."

"Have fun—and I hope you beat the pants off of the adults at Scrabble." Emily brushed a kiss across the top of Zoe's head and went out the door.

CHAPTER 9

"**G**ardenias!" Emily buried her nose in the fragrant bouquet. "I love gardenias."

"Good—I'm glad you like them. The lady at the florist shop suggested them. I was going to buy roses, but they didn't have much smell to them."

"The ones grown in commercial greenhouses usually don't," Emily said, stepping back from her door. "Let me put these in water and then we can go."

"Can I help?"

"Nope," Emily said, opening a cupboard and removing a pitcher. "I've got this." She placed her finger inside the pitcher and filled it until water reached her fingertip. She removed the cellophane from around the flowers, put them in the pitcher, and placed it on the counter to the right of her sink. "My entire apartment will smell heavenly by the time we get back. Thank you."

"You're welcome."

Emily put Garth into his working harness.

Grant helped her with her coat.

"Where are we going?" Emily asked as she pulled her mass of auburn curls from the collar of her coat.

"I made reservations at my favorite little neighborhood bistro. The food is excellent, and it's quiet there. They'll let you have a table as long as you want and no one tries to hustle you along. We can relax and talk. I'm excited to hear about this new initiative you're planning to propose at work."

"I'm eager to get your input." She gave Garth the forward command, and they set off. "I feel like I'm ninety percent there, with my proposal, but something's missing."

Grant cut his eyes to Emily. "I'm not sure that I'll have anything insightful to add, but I'm happy to listen."

"Don't sell yourself short," Emily said. "I've already learned that you're a strategic thinker."

Grant opened the front passenger door for Emily and the rear one for Garth. "Sometimes it's very helpful to talk something out with another person. Even if they have nothing to add, you gain perspective by articulating your thoughts."

"Exactly." Emily settled into her seat as Grant drove the short distance to the bistro. "Did Sylvia and Diedre have a nice time at the shower?"

"They did! You should have heard my mom. She raved about everything." He touched Emily's arm. "You made quite a favorable impression."

Emily felt her cheeks flush. "Your mom is so nice. I really like her." She paused, then continued. "What about Diedre? Did she say anything?"

"She had fun."

"Is that all she said?"

"She mentioned she got upset when the dog knocked her plate into her lap. But she said Sylvia helped her clean up, and it was fine."

"Anything else?"

Grant sucked in a deep breath. "You mean, did she mention Zoe?"

"Yes."

"Well—actually—she thinks Zoe doesn't like her."

"Oh, gosh. That's not true!"

"I told her that. Did Zoe say anything about Diedre?"

"Just that she thinks Diedre doesn't like her." Emily groaned.

"And that's not true, either." Grant stopped and put on his left turn blinker. He sighed heavily. "Kids—they're tough, aren't they?"

"They sure are."

"The more that a parent—or guardian—tells a kid that something isn't true, the more they think the opposite." He completed his turn into the parking lot and pulled up to the valet.

They got out of the car, retrieving Garth from the back seat.

"I don't know what we should do about this," Grant said. "I think it's all a big misunderstanding."

"I'm sure you're right," Emily said. "I mentioned Zoe's feelings to my mom, and she said to stay out of it. She believes these things usually work themselves out and I need to leave it alone. Learning about other people is part of the curriculum of growing up."

"Your mother sounds very wise," Grant observed. "That must be where you get it from."

They approached the hostess and were shown immediately to their table. Grant read the menu to Emily and after debating the merits of the cauliflower steak entrée or the beef short ribs, they both ordered the daily special of halibut served on a bed of puréed carrots.

The server brought them each a salad of arugula and heirloom tomatoes, topped with burrata and dressed with balsamic vinaigrette.

"So... we'll leave the issue of our girls aside for the moment, as your mom suggests. Tell me about this proposal that you're formulating at work."

Emily set her fork on her plate. "Let me back up and give you some context." She explained her meeting with Dhruv and her further investigation of his ideas. "The more I think about it, the more convinced I am that his ideas will address critical risks for our company."

"You've mentioned that he's brilliant, but he's not a good communicator."

"That's right. His strong suit isn't weaving his way through company politics."

"That's your forte."

"Maybe. I guess we're going to find out. As I said, this is going to be a delicate matter to propose."

The server cleared their empty salad plates and put their entrées in front of them. "Please enjoy."

"Tell me, again, about your corporate structure. You said that your boss's boss's boss…" His phone chimed. "It's Diedre," he said. "I'd better take this."

Emily nodded.

Grant tapped the screen of his phone. "Hi, honey? Everything okay?"

Emily took a bite of her fish.

"You were fine when I dropped you off. How can you suddenly feel so sick?" He listened. "Maybe you just need a drink of water and to lie down for a few minutes. Why don't you ask her mother…" He sighed heavily as he listened. "But you don't really want to come home. You've been looking forward to this all week. Give it some time—see if you feel better. I bet you will."

Emily patted her lips with her napkin and set it on the table.

"We just got our food. Why don't you give it another hour? If you still want to come home, you can call me and I'll pick you up after I take Emily home." His voice was even and reassuring. "You feel like you're going to throw up?" His voice now sounded resigned. "Get yourself to a bathroom and I'll pick you up as soon as I drop Emily off. See you soon." He disconnected the call. "I'm sorry, Emily."

"I heard. Of course you have to go."

Grant waved his hand to signal the server. "We'll have them box our food. At least you'll have your dinner."

"Why don't you just go? Now. Feeling like you're going to throw up is the worst and she'll hate being sick around her friends. As we said earlier, girls this age are tricky. I can take a rideshare home. No problem. I'll get the check, too."

"Absolutely not," Grant said. "On both counts. I'm not so sure that she's really sick. I've got no choice but to believe her, but I won't leave you in the lurch. Thank you for offering."

Their server approached their table. "We've had a sudden change of plans," Grant said, handing the man his credit card. "Can we get these to go?"

"Of course, sir," the server said.

Ten minutes later, Grant pulled to the curb in front of Emily's apartment building.

Emily and Garth were out of the car before Grant reached her door. She put her hand on his arm. "Garth and I can take it from here. I think you should go to Diedre. She'll be getting anxious."

Grant handed Emily a takeout bag. "Can you manage this? It has your dinner in it."

"Absolutely. Don't worry about me."

"All right, then. I'll be off. Thank you for being so under-standing, Emily."

"You're a parent—she has to come first."

Grant leaned in and kissed her briefly. "This will have to hold us."

Emily brushed his cheek with her hand. "Let me know how she is."

"Will do. And I want to finish our discussion about your proposal."

"I'd like that."

"I'll call you. Tomorrow." Grant retreated to his car as Garth and Emily made their way into their building.

CHAPTER 10

"Hey, you," Gina said into her phone. "I'm at our favorite coffee shop. They had three cinnamon rolls left, and I snagged them. Can I come over?"

"Sure." Emily chuckled. "I'll never say 'no' to those cinnamon rolls, but don't you want to take them to Craig?"

"Three rolls, two people? That's a formula for a fight over dividing up the third one. I figured it was a sign from the universe that I should bring them to you and Zoe. Besides, I want to hear about your date with Grant."

"There's not much to tell."

"What?"

"I'll fill you in when you get here."

"Be there in five."

Emily went to Zoe's room and pushed the door open slowly. She stood in the doorway, listening to the rhythmic breathing of the little girl she loved like a daughter. Zoe had been having such a good time playing Scrabble with Stephanie and Dhruv that she'd allowed Zoe to stay up far past her bedtime. But she didn't want Zoe to sleep so late that she wouldn't be able to go to bed on time tonight. Starting the week off on a bad night's sleep was never a good idea.

Emily made her way into the living room and listened to the time on her phone. She could let Zoe have another half hour. That would give Emily time to tell Gina about Grant without Zoe hearing her concerns.

Zoe knew that Emily had gone out with Grant, but it was early days in her relationship with him. Emily didn't want Zoe to worry about her and Grant. The girl had been through so much change and sorrow in her young life, with the deaths of her parents in a car accident and the recent passing of her grandmother.

The buzzer sounded. Emily pressed the button to allow Gina into the lobby, then flung the door wide. She heard Gina approach and put her fingers to her lips. "Zoe is still asleep," she whispered.

"She's starting to act like a teenager—sleeping until all hours." Gina kept her voice low. "I remember how we slept until noon."

"I know. It drove Mom crazy. She said I was wasting the best part of the day."

"I couldn't sleep that late now, if I tried."

"Same here. If I'm in bed until six, it's a miracle." Emily led them to a small round table underneath a window in the far corner of the living room. "Making sure Garth can go out

47

when he needs to is the most important reason for me to get up." Emily lowered herself into one chair flanking the table.

"This is such a pleasant, sunny spot," Gina said, placing a paper tray containing two cups of coffee and a box with the cinnamon rolls onto the table. "They gave me plenty of napkins. Do you want me to get us plates and forks?"

Emily was already pulling an enormous cinnamon roll out of the box. "They're still warm." She moaned as she took a large bite. "The icing is the perfect amount of gooey. If you want a plate and fork, go for it. I'm going to wolf mine down right now."

Gina sat with Emily as she helped herself to one of the delicious pastries. "No point in dirtying dishes," she said around a mouthful of the roll. "So—spill the beans. What happened last night?"

"Grant picked me up. He brought me those gardenias." Emily pointed over her shoulder toward the pitcher of flowers in her kitchen.

"They're gorgeous," Gina chimed in.

"He's so thoughtful. Anyway—he took me to a quiet bistro he likes so we could talk and linger as long as we wanted. He knew I wanted to pick his brain about a proposal I'm making at work."

"That all sounds great," Gina said, talking with her mouth full.

"I started filling him in over our salads and he was asking great questions. He's a good listener—I could tell that he was interested in what I was saying."

"Craig's like that, too. He never tunes me out when I'm

talking, even when it's about something he's not interested in."

"Connor was the opposite. If he cared about a topic, he was all in. But if he wasn't, I might as well have been talking to the wall."

"So... then what?"

"We'd no sooner gotten our entrées when Grant's cell phone rings and it's Diedre."

"Really? I thought she was going to a birthday party sleepover with her new friends from school. She told me all about it at the shower. Did something happen so she couldn't go?"

"No. Grant said the same thing—that she was super excited to go. He had dropped her off on the way to pick me up. We'd barely been at the restaurant for half an hour when Diedre called to say she wasn't feeling well and beg him to pick her up and take her home."

"This came up out of the blue?"

"According to Grant, yes."

"What was wrong with her?"

"She said she felt like throwing up."

"Hmmmm..."

"Maybe it was nerves—or one of the girls could have said something mean. You know how catty girls that age can be."

"Have you heard from Grant this morning?"

"He called while I was in the shower. He left a message that she was fine and to call him when I got a chance—that he'd love to finish our conversation from last night. I called back half an hour later and had to leave a voice mail for him."

Gina picked up her coffee and took a sip.

"I'm glad she's okay—of course. But I'm wondering if she was sick at all."

"What do you mean?"

"Did she know Grant had a date?"

"I'm not sure."

"Grant hasn't dated much since his wife died. Diedre may not want to share her dad."

"I thought of that," Emily said. "And I also think that she and Zoe aren't exactly friends. That may put a damper on things, too." She rested her elbows on the table and put her head in her hands. "The last thing either Grant or I need is trouble with our girls. They're adjusting to a new school, let alone the hormonal changes of pre-puberty. Maybe we should back away from a relationship before we get in too deep."

"You're a brilliant woman, Emily Main, but that is just plain stupid. You know how hard it is to find a great guy like Grant. I will not let you throw a chance at happiness away because of the antics of ten-year-old girls."

"I'm not sure what to do about any of this. Mom said we shouldn't try to force Zoe and Diedre to be friends."

"She's right. As for Diedre's reservations about Grant's dating? He'll have to deal with that."

"What if he doesn't see it?"

"Craig can talk to his brother about that. As for the girls —you leave them to me."

Emily swiveled her face to Gina's. "How on earth are you going to do anything about the girls?"

Both women turned toward the hallway as Zoe's bedroom door opened.

"Hey, sunshine," Gina called to her. "I've got a surprise for you."

"Gina?" Zoe skipped into the room. "Why are you here?"

"Two reasons," Gina said. "First—I brought each of us a cinnamon roll."

"I love those!"

Gina opened the box. "Help yourself."

Zoe lifted the roll over her head and licked up the icing that had run down the sides.

"The second thing is that I wanted to ask if you would be a junior bridesmaid in my wedding?"

Zoe sucked in a big breath. "You mean it?" she asked in a rush.

"I sure do. You'll have to get a fancy dress, and on the day before the wedding you'll have to skip school to get a mani and pedi with Emily and me. Plus, get your hair done the day of the wedding. Do you think you can tolerate all of that?"

"Sure!"

"Then it's settled. Thank you. We'll have to go dress shopping soon—next weekend, actually. With the other junior bridesmaid."

"Who's that?" Zoe asked.

"I haven't asked her yet. You were first. I'll let you know when she's said 'yes.'"

"I'm going to get a glass of milk," Zoe said, moving toward the kitchen.

"Gina." Emily leaned toward her, speaking in a whisper. "The other junior bridesmaid is Diedre?"

"Yes," Gina breathed.

"Are you out of your mind? You acted on impulse, asking her. What if your scheme to get the girls together doesn't work? I don't want you ruining your wedding."

"I like to think of it as divine inspiration. Quit fretting. Aunt Gina has a few tricks up her sleeve."

CHAPTER 11

*D*hruv stood in the doorway to Emily's office, shifting from foot to foot.

Emily had her back to him as her fingers tapped at her keyboard. "Dhruv?"

"Yes. How'd you know?"

Emily spun her chair around to face him. "Garth's tail," she said. "He doesn't wag it like that for anyone else here."

Dhruv chuckled.

"What's up?"

"Mike says he saw your boss in your office with you this morning," Dhruv said.

"That's right. He was in the city and stopped in."

"Well... What did he say?"

"About...?"

"The cybersecurity program we can write."

"He only dropped by for a few minutes. He had a meeting upstairs—that's why he was here. He just wanted to say 'hi.' "

"Did you mention our program?" He began walking back and forth from the door to her desk.

"I tried to," Emily said. "He was in a hurry and didn't have time to hear me out."

"So send him my memo."

"I brought that up." She pointed to the chair across the desk from her. "Sit. You make me nervous when you pace."

Dhruv sat, settling himself at the edge of the chair.

Emily blew out a breath. "I hate to say this, but he wasn't the least bit interested."

Dhruv leaned forward. "What did he say?"

"Cybersecurity is way outside our wheelhouse. We're the top programming team in the company and we've got more than enough work supporting our core functions."

"We talked about how we can continue with our current responsibilities and take this on, too."

"He wasn't interested, Dhruv."

"That's it?"

"He told me I could send him the memo, and he'd try to find time to look at it after the end of the quarter."

Dhruv remained silent, rocking back and forth in his seat. "We need to send it to someone else?"

"You mean go behind his back?"

"It's not behind his back. You went to him first, and he said 'no.' He's wrong, so we need to go to someone else."

Emily fought the smile seeking to force itself onto her

lips. This was the tenacious, don't-take-no-for-an-answer Dhruv who had refused to give up on her after she'd lost her eyesight—even when she'd given up on herself.

"I'm not sure that would be wise. And I have no idea who I would send it to."

"Howard Kent."

"Why?"

"You remember him, don't you? He was the EVP who attended your presentation when you found the glitch in the software update. He was extremely impressed with you."

"He was very gracious and said he wanted to find out more about the Foundation for the Blind."

"Exactly. Contact him."

"But this proposal has nothing to do with the Foundation. And he's at the top of the corporate ladder. This project is way below his level."

"Doesn't matter. Our whole industry is at serious risk of cyberattacks. He'll know that and understand how critical it is for us to protect the company."

"Well… you might be right."

"I am right. Send it to him."

Emily shook her head from side to side. "You've got the bit between your teeth and you won't let go, will you?"

"I don't know what you're talking about. Send it."

"I'll think about it," Emily said. "If I do, I'm going to have to craft an artfully worded email. In the meantime, I've got to finish the report I was working on."

Dhruv rose from the chair and walked to the door. He

turned back to her, resting his forearm on the door frame. "Do that email soon. It's a matter of when—not if—we're attacked."

CHAPTER 12

"We're going to spend all day together, aren't we, Zoe?" Gina turned to Emily while Zoe shuffled from side to side.

"All day dress shopping?" Emily asked. "Are you sure you don't want me to come with you?"

"Nope. My junior bridesmaids and I have got this. We'll buy dresses and have lunch. If we have time, we'll go to a matinee movie or get our nails done or something. This is a girls' day for the three of us."

"Sounds fun," Emily said, setting her laptop on the sofa and unwinding herself from her perch. She made her way to her purse, hanging from its usual spot on a hook by the door. Emily dug out her wallet and removed four bills that were all purposefully folded in half lengthwise, then folded in half lengthwise again. She held the money out to Gina. "I'll pay you back for the dress, but this should cover lunch and whatever else you do."

"Put that eighty dollars away," Gina said. "Today is my treat."

"You knew it was eighty?"

"I learned how bills are folded for the blind," Gina said quietly.

Emily tucked the bills back into her wallet. "Thank you. It means a lot to me that you're interested."

"If it's helpful to you, it's important to me. And now, we'd better be on our way. We're meeting the other junior bridesmaid at Nordstrom. Her dad is dropping her off." Gina leaned in and hugged Emily.

"Who's the other junior bridesmaid?" Zoe tugged on Gina's sleeve.

"Don't you want to be surprised?" Gina asked.

Zoe shook her head vigorously from side to side. "I want to know."

"It's Diedre Johnson."

Zoe's spine stiffened and she took a step back.

"You're not still upset about what happened at my shower, are you? That's been long forgotten."

Zoe remained silent, rooted to the spot.

Emily reached out and put her arm around Zoe's shoulder. "What is it, honey? Why don't you like Diedre?"

Zoe didn't answer.

"Has something happened at school? Is Diedre mean to you?" Gina asked.

"No. It's not her."

"Then what is it?"

"It's me." Zoe said softly. "Diedre's one of the popular girls. She's pretty—I'm not. I'm tall and skinny and I have fuzzy hair." She picked up a hank of her unruly dark curls. "Nothing's going to look good on me."

"That's not true," Emily began before Zoe cut her off.

"You can't see me. How would you know?"

Emily sucked in a breath.

"I'm sorry, Emily." Zoe's voice cracked. "That was so mean."

Gina swept them both into a group hug. She leaned back and smoothed Zoe's hair off of her forehead. "Here's the thing, Zoe. You are beautiful. Everyone sees it except you."

"We've all felt awkward and insecure in our appearances when we were growing up," Emily added. "I remember when Gina didn't want to go to the junior prom because her hair didn't turn out."

Gina threw back her head and laughed. "I'd forgotten about that." She spoke to Zoe. "Emily tried to curl it with a curling iron and ended up singeing an entire section of hair by my face."

"The burnt hair stank to high heaven. I still feel bad about that."

"What did you do?" Zoe asked, looking between Gina and Emily.

"We piled it all on top of my head in a ridiculous-looking updo."

"And you went to the dance?"

"I did," Gina said. "And had a great time." She paused. "I'll bet Diedre's feeling anxious and uncomfortable about today, too."

"You think so?"

Emily and Gina both nodded in unison.

"The best way to tackle nerves and insecurities is to start moving," Gina said. "Let's head out. Who knows? Maybe you and Diedre will end the day by being great friends. Like Em and me."

"Fat chance," Zoe mumbled, her face to the floor.

"Does Diedre know Zoe is the other junior bridesmaid?" Emily whispered in Gina's ear.

Gina shook her head no. "Don't worry," she whispered back.

"Have fun," Emily said. "I'll be here all day."

"It's beautiful out, Em. At least it will be until late afternoon, when it's supposed to rain. Why don't you and Garth go out and do something?"

"I'm working on a... delicate email and proposal for work."

"When are you ever not working?" Gina chastised. "Put that stupid laptop away and have a relaxing Saturday."

"I agree," Zoe, who had been waiting patiently by the door, chimed in. "It's supposed to rain tomorrow and I've got a book to read for school. You can do your work stuff then."

"All right, you two. I promise Garth and I will go for a long walk. Now—you'd better get going. You've got a lot to do today."

CHAPTER 13

*L*ight from high overhead halogens glinted off the marble floor. Upbeat jazz played softly in the background and was punctuated by snippets of excited conversation from other shoppers. Gina spotted Grant and Diedre waiting at the top of the escalator. She raised her hand over her head in greeting as she motioned for Zoe to step onto the moving steps.

Grant smiled and nodded in acknowledgment.

Diedre turned her head away when she saw them.

Gina and Zoe were carried to the second floor. Zoe took a giant step off the escalator and stood rigidly next to Grant.

"Sorry if you were waiting for us," Gina said, joining Grant.

"You're right on time!" He tapped his watch. "We got here a few minutes early."

Diedre and Zoe stood on either side of Grant and Gina, their faces pointed to the floor.

Grant caught Gina's eye over the top of the girls' heads and grimaced.

Gina mouthed the words, "I've got this," and winked at him.

"Being a junior bridesmaid is a big, grown-up thing to do. I'm so glad you both agreed." Gina opened her arms wide and gathered both girls around her. "We've got a lot of work to do today. My wedding is only a month away. We need to accomplish our mission today. Are you with me?"

Both girls turned their faces to her and nodded their agreement.

Gina gave Grant a dismissive nod of her head and he retreated with a mumbled, "have fun."

"My wedding will be outside—on a cliff overlooking the ocean. I'm praying we have good weather. It'll be breezy, for sure, so you'll either want sleeves or we'll get a wrap to go over your dresses."

Zoe and Diedre nodded solemnly.

"I think a soft teal blue will look good on both of you. Is that all right?"

Again, both girls nodded.

"I thought we'd shop in the teen department. Everything in the girls' department is too babyish." Gina smiled inwardly at the expressions of pleasure that now emanated from the girls.

"All three of us are going to sift through the fancy dresses in this department." She gestured to the area behind her.

"Pick out any dress you think you'd like so we can try it on. Just stick with light teal blue. It's a popular color this season and there's lots to choose from."

"What size do you think we'd be?" Diedre asked, lifting her chin to look at Zoe, who was a head taller than she was.

Gina pursed her lips as she looked at the two girls. "I think you'll be a small, Diedre. Zoe is tall for her age. I think she'll need a large so we have enough length. We'll have them tailored, so don't worry if something is big. If you find a dress you like, grab it in a small and a large."

Diedre headed for a rack of dresses against the wall while Zoe stuck with Gina.

"Don't you want to look for dresses? You were so good at it when we shopped with Martha and Emily."

Zoe shrugged. "I like shopping for other people."

"Not yourself?"

Zoe nodded.

"Why?"

She shrugged again. "I know what you and Emily said about me being beautiful, but nothing looks good on me."

Gina stopped suddenly and faced Zoe. "Honey—that's simply not true. You're tall—all the famous models are tall. Clothes just naturally look better on you tall gals. Plus, your eyes are huge and dark and gorgeous. I'll bet you won't need makeup when you're my age. You're not pale and pasty, like me. I'd kill to have your coloring."

Zoe raised her eyes to Gina. "Really?"

"Yes, really." Gina put her arm around Zoe's shoulder and hugged her briefly. "You're a stunner, honey. Now—let's get busy." She pointed to a tiny figure in the distance carrying an armload of dresses. "Diedre's way ahead of us."

Gina and Zoe weaved their way through the department, methodically sliding hangers along racks, contemplating anything that might be a possibility.

Zoe selected a simple A-line and a satin jumpsuit.

Gina scooped up two lace-covered dresses and one in cut velvet.

"Diedre texted me," Gina said. "She's waiting for us by the dressing rooms." She led the way and a salesperson placed them in the largest fitting room.

"I can see that you ladies have a lot of work to do. You must be shopping for a very special occasion?" She raised an eyebrow at Gina.

"These are my junior bridesmaids," Gina said.

The woman beamed. "What a happy thing! You've picked some lovely dresses. I'm going to bring another chair in here for you. Would anyone like a bottle of water?"

All three nodded 'yes' and the woman left them.

"Woah," Zoe said. "That's so fancy."

"I love coming here," Diedre said. "My mom always shopped at Nordstrom." Sadness seized her features.

Gina and Zoe glanced at each other.

"You start," Zoe said. "Which one is your favorite? Let's try that one on first."

Diedre pulled a lace dress with a full skirt from the sea of dresses hung neatly on a bar running the length of the wall. "This one, with the big skirt," she said. "I loved twirling in dresses like this when I was little." She slipped out of her T-shirt and jeans and pulled the dress on over her head.

Gina secured the zipper.

The cloud that had fallen on Diedre's features when she'd mentioned her late mother vanished. She turned this way and that in front of the three-way mirror in the dressing room, admiring the dress. She finished with a quick twirl.

"You like that one, don't you?" Gina asked.

"I love it!"

Gina smoothed the fabric over Diedre's shoulders as she stared at the girl's reflection in the mirror. "It's a perfect fit. We wouldn't have to do anything to it." She pulled the dress in the large size from its hanger and handed it to Zoe. "Let's see what you think of it."

Zoe shucked her outer garments and put on the dress. The length was right, but she swam in it.

Gina positioned Zoe in front of the mirror and pulled the fabric close to her body from behind. "This is what it would look like when alterations are done. They'd have a lot to cut down, but they could do it." She met Zoe's eyes in the mirror. "Let's see what else might work," Gina said, quickly undoing Zoe's zipper.

"We can still choose this one, can't we? If we don't like another one as well?" Diedre asked.

"Of course. We're going to try all of them on, so we make the best choice. The only thing I ask is that you both wear the same dress."

The girls got busy, stepping in and out of dresses as Gina handed them garments, zipped and unzipped, and replaced garments on hangers. By the time they were done, two top choices hung on one end of the bar, separate from the other dresses. They could not have been more different.

"So," Gina said, looking at the girls. "We've got that first lace dress that Diedre likes and the satin jumpsuit that Zoe favors. If we get the lace dress, Zoe's will need a lot of alteration. If we choose the jumpsuit, the same will be true of Diedre's."

"Which one do you like best?" Zoe asked Gina.

"I think you'll both look fabulous in either one." Gina bit her lip. "To be honest, I'm more of a traditionalist. For a wedding—my wedding—I prefer the lace dress."

Diedre clasped her hands together. Zoe glanced at her feet, then looked up. "Let's get the lace one, then."

"Are you sure you don't mind?" Gina asked.

Zoe's lips set into a line. "No. It's fine. It's your wedding."

"Thank you, honey," Gina said. "I'm going to ring for the alterations lady and we'll get this marked before we head for lunch. After lunch, we'll go to a movie or get manis and pedis. You get to choose, Zoe." She pushed a buzzer on the wall as Zoe wriggled back into the dress.

CHAPTER 14

*H*ad I heard my name and the word "walk" mentioned in the same sentence? I certainly hoped so.

Emily had taken me to my area out back when we first got up—the spot that was regularly used by Sabrina, Biscuit, and me. And our friends Sugar and Rocco. They lived in our building with Dhruv. The sun was cutting through the fog and it looked like it was going to be a fine day.

I loved walking in the sun. I also loved walking in the rain. I even enjoyed snow, as long as I had my boots on. You could say that I loved to walk.

I'd come to realize that most people longed for the weekend and hated Monday morning when they had to go back to work. It was the opposite for me. I looked forward to Mondays when we were up and out early, and on the move all week. Lying in my bed most of the weekend while Emily typed on her laptop and Zoe sprawled on her bed, reading, got boring for me.

I pranced over to Emily and pushed my muzzle into her hand.

She reached over and stroked the top of my head. "You heard us, didn't you? We'll go as soon as I finish. I just have a couple more points to add."

Her phone chirped and announced that Grant was calling. Emily lunged for it.

"Good morning. How are you?" His low, rich rumble made her pulse race.

Emily listened. "I'm good. They just left. I'm doing some work stuff."

She was quiet and listened for a long time.

"I'd love to. That's a great idea. I can finish this up tomorrow." She fell silent again, holding the phone to her ear.

"Garth will adore that!"

My ears perked up.

"See you in ten. I'll get my shoes on and Garth and I will be waiting out front."

I raced to the door, my tail wagging at full speed. I didn't know what we were going to do, but I knew it involved Emily and me going out. An adventure with my Emily was always my favorite way to spend the day.

CHAPTER 15

 rant spotted the woman with the mane of auburn hair waiting on the sidewalk, her black lab in working harness at her side. He sprinted the remaining half block between them.

"Good morning, you two," he called as he reached them.

Emily turned toward the familiar voice and smiled. "Good morning, yourself. I'm intrigued by your invitation. Where are you taking us?"

"If I told you now, it wouldn't be a surprise, would it?"

"So that's how you're going to play it?"

"I'm afraid so."

"Am I dressed appropriately for the occasion?"

"Light jacket; sensible walking shoes. Yep. You're ready." He leaned in and kissed her cheek. "I parked my car on the next block—to your left."

Emily turned. "Forward," she commanded Garth, and

they began walking. "You called right after Gina and Zoe arrived at Nordstrom?"

"Yep."

"How did that go? Were the girls okay with each other?"

"Of course they were," Grant said.

"No tension?"

Grant cleared his throat. "None that Gina can't handle."

"Oh, boy." Emily stopped walking and touched Grant's arm. "Maybe we shouldn't go gallivanting about the city— what if Gina's plan doesn't work, and she needs to pull the plug on this whole idea?"

"It's going to work," he said. "Both girls are good, decent people."

"That's true."

"So whatever is going on between them has to be based on an adolescent misunderstanding."

"I agree with that."

"Then let's allow them to have the necessary life experience of finding out that their preconceived idea about another person is wrong."

"You sound like my mom."

He took her free hand. They quickly crossed the remaining distance to his car. He opened the rear door for Garth and the front door for Emily. When they were all settled in, he turned to her.

"I have a request," he said.

"Sure."

"The only people on this date are you and me. And Garth,

of course. Let's leave Zoe and Diedre to Gina and spend our time getting to know each other."

Emily took his face in her hands and kissed him. "That sounds like a terrific idea. As of now, it's just us."

GRANT PULLED to the curb after a short drive along city streets. He helped Emily and Garth out of the car. "You get to pick—right or left," he said when Garth was in his harness and ready to work.

"We're going for a walk?"

"We are."

"But not a hike, I assume."

"No. I would have told you to wear hiking boots."

Emily stood still, listening.

"Do you want me to tell you where we are now?"

Emily shook her head. "Let me try to guess." She gave the forward command, and they took off. A light breeze lifted her hair from her collar. She pointed her face upward, enjoying the warmth of the sun on her face.

Grant walked beside her, letting the pair work.

"We're on a sidewalk," Emily said.

"We are."

"Garth is moving in a straight line. He doesn't have to go around any obstacles. I also don't hear a lot of traffic close by." She continued to walk. "I hear cars up ahead."

They came to a place where the sidewalk sloped downward and raised dots filled the concrete.

Garth stopped.

"We're at an intersection," Emily said. "I can hear cars. Garth is waiting."

"That's right."

"I know how to listen for the direction of the traffic before I cross a street, but you can tell us when we can cross," Emily said.

"We can cross now," Grant said. "I'm impressed with how well you two work together. Diedre's grandfather has a guide, and it's incredible to see them."

They crossed the street.

"Which way now?"

"Again, your choice."

"I think we'll go straight."

They walked for another few minutes. The high-spirited voices of children rang out up ahead, and the sound of a soccer ball being kicked.

"Any idea where we are?"

"We're in a residential neighborhood," Emily said.

"Very good," Grant replied.

"A very nice one, I'd say," Emily continued. "The sidewalks are in good shape—they're not full of cracks where tree roots have pushed them up. Traffic is light, and I think cars are coming out of driveways instead of being parked along the curb." She turned toward Grant. "How am I doing?"

"Brilliantly. You've nailed it. We're in one of my favorite neighborhoods in the city—where, one day, I'm going to buy a house."

"Ohhh... do tell. Where are we?"

"Presidio Heights."

Emily stopped abruptly. "Holy cow. We are in a nice neighborhood. You've got high aspirations."

"There's no point in aiming low."

"I've had lunch at several of the restaurants here. They're terrific. Since I can't see the beautiful homes, why don't you tell me about them as we walk?"

"I'd love to. On one condition."

"Name it."

"As an architect, I can talk about this neighborhood all day. Promise me you'll tell me when you've heard enough. I don't want to bore you to death and my internal filter on this topic is... well... unreliable."

Emily laughed. "I don't think you have anything to worry about."

"Even so..."

"I promise."

Grant began describing the homes they passed—the styles and incongruous details that added to the distinctive charm of the area. He pointed out the 1909 red and black Tudor-inspired mansion known as the Roos House, noting that it was one of architect Bernard Maybeck's masterpieces. "The house was modified in its early days by Maybeck, himself, and remains true to his design."

"Have you been inside?"

"I toured it during architecture school. Every detail was attended to by the architect. The redwood walls were sculptural works of art. The whole place had been impeccably maintained, too."

"Maybe you'll make your mark on the city with your work, just like he did."

"That's my dream," he replied. "Maybeck also was part of the group of architects who designed the Swedenborgian Church."

"I've been to a wedding there—before I lost my eyesight. Those huge beams in that vaulted, coffered ceiling are spectacular."

They continued their ramble up and down the hilly sidewalks.

"The landscaping on these homes is an integral part of their beauty," Grant continued. "A good landscape architect can frame the structure with serene, sculpted monochrome tones or draw the eye with an explosion of color."

"I can see fuzzy clouds of vivid colors."

Grant stepped ahead of her. "Follow me," he said, opening a low iron gate and leading Emily and Garth up a flagstone pathway toward steps to a front door.

"Why do I have the feeling we're going somewhere we're not supposed to?"

"Just a few more steps. We'll be outta here before anyone notices us." He stopped walking and put his hands on her shoulders, turning her a quarter turn. "Look down."

Emily gasped. "It's bright orange!"

"That's right."

She reached out her free hand to touch the bush covered in a profusion of tiny orange blossoms. "What is this?"

"Lantana. Always a prolific bloomer and almost impossible to kill."

"Sounds like a good choice for our climate."

"It's one of my favorites. We'll—you'll—want them when you have a house."

Emily kept her face down and ran her hand across the top of the bush, wondering if he'd meant to refer to their house.

"We'd better get back to the public sidewalk," he said, leading the way as they retraced their steps.

A woman walking a dog passed them going the other direction, murmuring a pleasant, "Good morning." Children riding bikes on the other side of the street called to each other.

Emily paused and hugged herself. "I can feel why you love this place. There's a happy vibe of everyday activity. It's full of gorgeous homes, but it's not a place where showy people come to live the high life."

"Exactly. This is a family neighborhood where people come to put down roots. There are high-end shops and fabulous restaurants, but no night clubs and trend-of-the-moment bars. People here want to walk their dogs, be good neighbors, and live quiet lives."

"That's very inviting. I love my neighborhood, but it's a lot more congested—more urban—than this one," Emily said. "I have a feeling you're going to make your dream come true."

Grant circled Emily with his arms and drew her to him.

"Thank you," he said, resting his chin on top of her head, "for not scoffing at me and telling me this is out of reach."

"Never," she said. "I'm a sky's-the-limit kind of gal."

"I've kept you walking for over two hours," Grant said. "I think I'd better get the two of you some nourishment." He named a restaurant. "How about we grab a fashionably late lunch there?"

"Are you kidding? They've been written up in all the foodie magazines. I've been dying to try it."

"We're right down the street," Grant said. "And I know they're very accommodating to guide dogs. I've been there with Diedre's grandfather. Garth will have water before we do."

"As it should be," Emily said. "Let's go."

CHAPTER 16

"*I*'m going to the ladies' room," Gina said to Diedre and Zoe as they selected a table at the Nordstrom café. "I'll be right back."

Diedre picked up her drink and took a sip. "This has been fun. I can't wait for the wedding."

Zoe nodded. "It's really nice of Gina. You're gonna look beautiful in that dress."

"I love it. Thanks for going with it. You're gonna look amazing too."

Zoe rolled her eyes. "As if."

"What do you mean? They'll fix it—you heard what the alterations lady said."

Zoe shrugged. "I'll never be as pretty as you and Gina."

Diedre hesitated before leaning across the table toward Zoe. "That's not true at all, Zoe." She set her drink on the table. "I think you're so pretty." She narrowed her eyes as she looked at Zoe. "You don't feel good in that dress, do you?"

Zoe shook her head.

"I've read stories about bridesmaids who hate the dresses they have to wear." She drew in a deep breath. "That sucks."

Zoe looked at her plate.

"No," Diedre stated simply. "That's not going to happen here. Not the first time you're a bridesmaid. We're going to tell Gina that we've changed our mind and we're going with the jumpsuit."

Zoe raised her chin quickly. "But they've already pinned my alterations."

"So what? They haven't started on them yet. We'll tell Gina when she gets back from the ladies' room and she can call alterations. Tell them to stop."

"You'd do that? For me?"

"You won't have fun in that dress."

"But you hate the jumpsuit. It'll be the same for you." Zoe paused, thinking, then snapped her fingers. "I've got it. We'll convince Gina that we don't have to match."

"I'm not sure she'll go for that."

"Leave it to me," Zoe said, tapping into her characteristic determination. "I'll convince her. She won't mind—when she hears me out."

Diedre lifted her eyes above Zoe's shoulders to the figure of the woman approaching. "Here she comes." Diedre grinned at Zoe. "Good luck. And if Gina says 'no,' we're wearing the jumpsuit."

"I've got this," Zoe whispered conspiratorially as Gina slid into her chair.

CHAPTER 17

Garth led Emily and Grant to her front door.

"Gina should be here with the girls any minute," Emily said, unlocking the door and ushering them inside. "I hope we're doing the right thing— you being here when Gina drops them off."

"It would be silly to make Gina go out of her way to bring Diedre to my house when I'm at your place now. Why should I race out of here to be home before they arrive?"

"Because then we can hide the fact that we went out today."

Grant circled Emily with his arms and drew her close. "I don't want to keep it a secret. In case you haven't noticed," he said, brushing kisses along her jawline, "I'm falling for you, Emily Main."

Emily shivered with pleasure and gave herself to the

depth of his kiss as his mouth found hers. When their lips parted, she took a step back.

"I think we'd better take things slowly. Being 'us' could be complicated. Our kids don't like each other…"

"Gina may have changed all that," Grant interrupted.

"And even if they now get along, that doesn't mean Diedre or Zoe are ready for us to date."

Grant ran his hands down her arms. "It's not up to them. We're the adults here—we're in charge of our lives. We have to be cautious and make good choices about who we go out with, but we don't need—and shouldn't ask—for their approval."

"You think so?"

"I do. Kids don't want to be in charge, no matter how much they try to be. They want us, as parents, to set the tone. If I'm happy in my life, that sets a good example for Diedre, too."

"I agree with that. I just hope we don't have a rocky road with these two."

He squeezed her hand. "If we do, we'll figure out how to handle them. Together."

Emily opened her door and led him to the sofa.

"I meant to ask," Grant said, as they settled down to wait for the girls, "what did you do about that proposal you were going to make at work?"

Emily filled him in on her brief meeting with her boss and Dhruv's suggestion that she go over his head.

"I think Dhruv's right. What have you got to lose?"

"My boss might get mad?"

"It's not like you didn't bring it to him. He didn't tell you to drop it."

"That's what I've concluded. I was working on an email to the EVP when you called this morning." She pulled her laptop off the coffee table. "Would you mind looking at it? I'd really appreciate your honest opinion."

"I'd love to." Grant leaned over her shoulder as the screen reader feature helped her navigate to the draft email. He read the email, scrolling down the page, then read it a second time. "This is really good."

"Thanks. Any suggestions?"

"A couple. May I?" He slid the laptop onto his lap and typed. The screen reader feature read his changes. "What do you think?"

"I like it! You've clarified a couple of things and smoothed one of my transitions."

"Are you going to send it?"

Emily's hand hovered over the keypad, then she tapped send. "There! For better or worse, it's done. I'll stop thinking about it. And I can tell Dhruv that I've sent it. You have no idea how tenacious he is."

"From what you've told me about him, I have an idea. I hope it works out for you, Em. I know you and your team would solve this problem if given the chance."

Emily leaned in to kiss him, when they were interrupted by a staccato burst of knocks on the door. "That'll be Zoe. She has the key code for the lobby door," she said, getting to her feet. "They're back. Ready?"

"Of course." He followed her to the door and pulled it open. "Well," he said with enthusiasm, "mission accomplished?"

"Dad! What are you doing here?"

"Emily and I spent the day together. We just got back, and I thought I'd save Gina the trip to our house to drop you off." He stepped back to allow them to enter the apartment.

"Did you find a dress?" Emily asked.

"We didn't find just one," Gina said. "They each found one that they absolutely love and that looks gorgeous on them."

"They're not going to match?"

"Nope. We started out that way, but Zoe convinced me it wasn't a good idea. They'll both be wearing the same color, but each girl got exactly what she wanted."

"I've got a satin jumpsuit instead of a dress," Zoe said. "Wanna see it?" Without waiting for a response, she began pulling the garment out of its cocoon of tissue paper inside a Nordstrom carrier bag. She held the jumpsuit up in front of her.

"Zoe rocks it," Diedre said.

"What's your dress look like?" Emily asked.

"It's lace, with a great big skirt."

"So pretty," Zoe supplied.

Grant brought his palms together and slid them against each other. "Sounds like today was a complete success. For all of us."

"It certainly was," Gina said.

"There's now only one thing left to do," Grant said.

"What's that?" Emily asked.

"Eat dinner. Anyone hungry? I'd like to take you all out. The girls can choose."

"Pizza!" they cried in unison.

"Is that okay with you, Em?"

"Sure."

"Gina—do you and that brother of mine have big plans tonight?"

"No. I figured today would be hectic. We were going to order in."

"Why don't you call Craig and ask him to meet us?"

"That sounds like fun. I left my phone in the car. I'll be right back."

"Wanna see my room real quick before we go?" Zoe asked Diedre.

"Sure."

The two girls disappeared down the hallway.

Grant and Emily threw their arms around each other.

"It all worked out!" Emily said. "Gina's a genius."

"And a wonderful friend," Grant replied.

The sound of high-spirited giggling reached them from Zoe's room.

When Gina reentered the apartment, she announced that Craig was on his way.

Grant and Emily turned to her, and the smiles on their faces told her everything she needed to know.

"Today has been a wonderful day," Emily said. "We don't know how to thank you, Gina."

"You don't have to. You've always been family to me, Em,

and Grant and I soon will be. I just want you to be happy." Her voice was thick with emotion. "I'm starved. Let's get this show on the road."

CHAPTER 18

*E*mily wiped the kitchen counter while Zoe put the milk back into the refrigerator. "You say you finished your book?"

"Yep. My report's all done."

"What would you like to do this afternoon? It's nasty outside. Garth loves the rain, but even he rushed to do his business when I took him out so he could get back inside."

"Can we bake cookies?"

"Perfect idea! What kind?"

"Chocolate chip. I know we have chips in the cupboard."

"We'll have everything else we need on hand. There's a recipe on the back of the package of chips." Emily located the canisters on the counter that were labeled flour and sugar. "Read the recipe to me."

Zoe retrieved the bags of chocolate chips and began reading. "One cup butter, three quarters cup firmly packed brown sugar, two large eggs." Zoe stopped abruptly. "We only have one egg."

"We can always cut the recipe in half," Emily said. "You can practice your math skills."

"Then we won't have as many cookies."

"That's true. Why don't we see if Stephanie has an egg we can borrow?"

"We're going to return an egg we put into cookies?"

Emily laughed. "We'd bring her an egg after we've been to the grocery store."

"Or we could give her some of our cookies," Zoe suggested.

"I'm sure she'd like that even better. Get the biggest bowl from the cupboard under the island and I'll text Stephanie."

Zoe found the bowl and set it near the canister of flour. "I'll get out the braille measuring cups and spoons, too."

"As soon as we hear from Stephanie—so we know if we're cutting the recipe in half or not—we can get started."

Emily's phone cheeped with an incoming text.

Zoe read out Stephanie's reply. "At Dhruv's. He has eggs. Come here to get one."

"I'll wait in the doorway while you go over to Dhruv's," Emily said.

"He's at the end of the hall," Zoe said. "You don't need to watch me. I'm not a baby."

"Even so, I'll listen from the doorway."

Zoe raced to the apartment at the far end of the hall and knocked. Dhruv opened the door.

Emily heard a snippet of an aria from an opera that she

didn't recognize. She smiled to herself. Dhruv loved to listen to opera on Sunday afternoons. Apparently Stephanie enjoyed it, too.

He held out an egg.

Zoe took it and headed back to her apartment without ever exchanging a word with him.

"You didn't say thank you and tell him you'll bring him some cookies," Emily chastised.

"I didn't need to," Zoe said. "I'm sure Dhruv knows. He senses stuff."

Emily chuckled as she closed the door behind them. "I guess that's true."

"Can I mix the butter, eggs, and sugars? Martha told me that's called 'creaming.' It's fun."

"Sure. Be sure to preheat the oven to 350 degrees. I'll measure and put the dry ingredients in the bowl." Emily ran her thumb over the raised dots on the handle of the largest measuring cup. "Three cups of flour, right?"

"Yep," replied Zoe.

Emily scooted the canister of flour to the edge of the sink. The lid wouldn't budge, so she pressed the canister against her chest and gave it a firm yank. The lid gave way suddenly, showering her with a cloud of flour.

"Aack," she sputtered, waving away flour dust from her face.

"That used to happen to my grandma, too."

Emily laughed. "This is why I *should* be wearing an apron." She dipped the measuring cup into the flour and brought it to the sink, leveling the flour with her fingers as the excess fell neatly into the sink. Emily tipped the cup of flour into the mixing bowl and repeated her actions two more times.

Rain lashed the kitchen window. Garth and Sabrina huddled together on the oversize dog bed in the corner of the living room.

"What was that music Dhruv was listening to? Like fancy music—with singers."

"That's called opera," Emily said.

"I couldn't understand the words."

"That's because it was being sung in a different language. That sounded like Italian."

"Are there ones in English?"

"Yes."

"It sounded really pretty in Italian."

"I agree. You don't need to understand the words to know what's going on in an opera."

"Can we listen to it while we work?"

"That would be lovely! Go to YouTube and search for Carmen. That's a very famous opera with gorgeous music."

The stirring "Toreador Song" soon filled the apartment. They stirred, scooped out dough, and put cookie sheets in the oven in seamless harmony while Bizet's masterpiece swirled around them.

By the time the second cookie sheet was out of the oven, Sabrina had abandoned her bed and skulked around their feet, hoping for dropped pieces of cookie dough.

The irresistible aroma of warm chocolate had even coaxed Garth into the kitchen.

"Can we try one?" Zoe asked.

"Let's get these last two trays of cookies into the oven and transfer the ones from the trays we just took out to the cooling racks. Then we can get glasses of milk and do a taste test."

"You don't want coffee?"

"Not for chocolate chip cookies, straight out of the oven. You have to have milk. It's mandatory."

They finished baking, sampling their creations, and cleaning up the kitchen as the opera reached its rousing conclusion.

"I don't think Carmen has a happy ending," Zoe said.

Emily blew out a breath. "No. You're right. It doesn't."

"It was still fun to listen to while we worked," Zoe said. "Can I take cookies to Dhruv and Stephanie now?"

"That would be nice."

"Is it okay if I stay and play Scrabble?"

"Only if they invite you." Emily listened to the time on her smart watch. "It's four. Can you be back by five? Text me when you leave so I can open the door and watch for you."

"Dhruv won't let me walk in the building alone," Zoe said. "Don't worry."

Emily helped Zoe stack a mound of warm cookies on a plate. "Have fun," she said as Zoe headed back down the hall. Emily hugged herself as she marveled at how rich her life had become.

"HI, ZOE," Stephanie called from the living room of Dhruv's apartment.

"How'd you know it was me?" Zoe joined her.

"I swear I smelled those cookies before Dhruv opened the door."

"They're so good. Want one?"

"I was going to say 'no'—it's too close to dinner—but I can't resist."

Dhruv sank down onto the sofa next to Stephanie, balancing a tall stack of cookies on top of a paper napkin. "Here," he said, passing a cookie to her, "I brought us a couple."

"If I know you, you've got way more than two of them," she addressed Zoe. "Am I right?"

Zoe giggled and squatted next to Biscuit, who was sprawled out on the floor by Stephanie, her nose high in the air, nostrils twitching at the heady aroma of warm chocolate. "She's not in her harness. Can I pet her?"

"Sure. She's not working right now."

Zoe rubbed between the yellow lab's ears and stroked down her back. Biscuit abandoned her quest for the source of the delicious smell and turned her snout to Zoe, giving her a smattering of doggy kisses.

"How was your shopping day with Gina?" Stephanie asked between bites.

"Super fun! You won't believe who the other junior bridesmaid is." Zoe recounted her day with Gina and Diedre while Stephanie and Dhruv worked their way through the stack of cookies.

"You're going to be part of a wedding party soon. That's very exciting!" Stephanie said.

"Have you ever been in a wedding?" Zoe asked.

"No. I always wanted to be, though." Stephanie tucked her feet up under her. "I'm an only child and neither of my parents have siblings, so I don't have any cousins. None of my close friends had weddings. It just never happened."

"How about you, Dhruv?" Zoe asked.

He shifted uncomfortably. "No—and I don't want to be. Indian weddings are long, drawn out, noisy affairs. I don't like even going to the wedding when one of my cousins gets married."

Stephanie straightened and twisted her upper body toward him.

"It's…" He paused, searching for words. "It's too much for me."

Stephanie ran her hand along his arm. "We've got an hour before we need to start supper. Why don't we all play Scrabble?"

CHAPTER 19

I gave myself a good shake, then moved my eyes
from Emily to Sabrina and back again. The heavy
rain of the afternoon had given way to a fine drizzle in the
evening. Now, during our final comfort break at bedtime,
only the grass was wet.

I'd marched right out the back door to my spot, made
short work of my business, and was ready to go inside for
my nighttime treat and my memory foam bed. Even though
I'd spent most of the day quietly inside—maybe *because* I'd
been inactive during this rainy day—I was tired and ready
for sleep.

Sabrina, on the other hand, was taking her sweet time.
Zoe was admonishing her to "do her business," but Sabrina
was snuffling the ground, searching for the perfect spot. I
loved my less disciplined flatmate, but this routine got
tiresome.

I shook again, jangling my collar. It was the only way I knew to signal my impatience.

Sabrina finally began to circle, and I knew we were finally getting somewhere when the back door opened and Sugar and Rocco raced out, followed by Dhruv.

Sabrina stopped in mid-circle as Sugar, the affable golden retriever, ran on by her, intent on doing her business and getting back inside. I liked Sugar—she had a good head on her shoulders.

Rocco was another story. In my experience, hounds—even tiny dachshunds like Rocco—were headstrong, opinionated, and unruly.

He made a beeline for Sabrina, barking his fool head off and nipping at her heels.

Sabrina jumped, and soon she and Rocco were chasing each other around the small grassy area.

This was not a good time to play. I sat down with a humph.

Sugar joined me, rather than enter into the ill-timed merriment. I liked that. She must have agreed with me.

"I've made a big mistake." Dhruv blurted out, waving his hands in front of him.

"What're you talking about? Is it something at work?" Emily asked.

"No. With Stephanie."

"I'm sure you didn't," Emily began.

"I did. You heard it, Zoe."

Zoe abandoned her attempts to make Sabrina stop

chasing Rocco and attend to the purpose of their trip to the grassy area. "You mean about not liking weddings?"

"Yes."

"Why is that a mistake?"

"I don't want a wedding, but I want to be married. They're different."

"That's true," Emily replied. "Was Stephanie upset?"

"I'm not sure."

"Did you think she was, Zoe?"

"No. But she said she likes weddings," Zoe said.

Dhruv groaned. "This isn't good."

"If you think there's a problem, Dhruv, you need to find out."

"We've never had a problem—not the whole time we've been together."

Emily felt him swaying as he transferred his weight from foot to foot. "It's normal to have misunderstandings and disagreements, Dhruv. All couples have them."

"What do I do?"

"You talk to her, Dhruv. Ask her how she's feeling. And— most importantly—listen to what she says. Don't be thinking of what you're going to say to her. Especially don't be thinking about how you're going to try to talk her out of how she's feeling."

"This relationship stuff is tricky."

Emily suppressed a smile. "It is—for everyone. You've got the biggest heart of anyone I know, Dhruv. Listen to her and be honest with each other." She reached out a hand and found his back. She rested it there, lightly. "You're going to be fine, Dhruv. You can do this."

"You think so?" His tone was plaintive.

"I'm positive."

Dhruv whistled for his dogs and turned abruptly, marching back into the building.

"Wow," Zoe said softly. "I hope Dhruv and Stephanie are gonna be okay."

"I'm sure they will be, honey," Emily replied. "Now—get that dog of yours to do her business so we can head inside and go to bed. I'm beat!"

I watched as Sabina finally finished the task at hand. We locked eyes as she trotted up to me and I knew we were thinking the same thing. It was good that we were out here when Dhruv had come out with our pals. He'd needed the conversation with Emily and Zoe. Sometimes an annoying delay is a fortuitous opportunity.

CHAPTER 20

"*N*ow?" Stephanie dictated the responsive text into her phone.

"Yes. Now." Her screen reader feature read Dhruv's text to her.

"It's so late. I'm already in bed."

"It has to be now."

"Okay."

"I'm right outside your door."

"Oh, for heaven's sake," Stephanie muttered as she put her phone onto her nightstand, stuffed her feet into her slippers, and slung her robe around her shoulders. "It's all right, Biscuit," she said as she passed her guide dog's bed. "I'll be right back."

She made her way easily to her door, every pathway in her apartment committed to muscle memory. Stephanie unhooked the security chain and turned the deadbolt back, opening the door.

Dhruv stepped quickly past her and stood in the faint light afforded by the ceiling fixtures in the hallway. He turned and stared at Stephanie; her face hidden in shadow.

"What's happened? Is something wrong?"

"I want to be married," he said. "I've always wanted a wife —and kids. I want a family. People to love," he continued in a rush.

"Okay. That's good to know."

"You need to know that."

"Thank you." She stood facing him, waiting for him to continue.

Dhruv remained silent.

"Is there more?"

"Yes."

Stephanie reached behind her, to the wall, and flipped on a light switch so Dhruv could see. "Come on in. We can't stand here in my doorway." She led him to the living room of her one-bedroom apartment.

"Do you want something to drink?" she asked, motioning toward the kitchen as they passed by.

"No."

She sat on the small sofa and Dhruv settled down next to her.

"I want to be married," he said.

"You've already said that."

"I want to be married to you."

Stephanie breathed in sharply.

"I love you, Stephanie." He took her hand in his. "I'm happy with you. Happy and comfortable. I look forward to every minute we spend together. I've never felt like this—in my whole life."

Tears puddled inside her lower lids.

"But it's not just about me. How do you feel?"

"Oh, Dhruv," Stephanie sputtered, her tears splashing onto their clasped hands. "I love you, too." She snuffled, trying to regain her composure.

"Do you want to be married to me?"

"Yes! Oh Dhruv, yes!" She flung her arms around his neck and tried to pull him to her.

"Then we have a problem."

"What would that be?"

"You want a wedding. You said so earlier. And I want you to have what you want. I understand that every woman dreams about their wedding. And you deserve one." His voice cracked as he continued. "I'm not sure I can go through with a ceremony—especially an Indian wedding like the ones my family has had."

Stephanie smoothed the hair from his forehead with tender hands. "Is that what you're worried about?"

"We can't *be* married if we don't *get* married. And you want a wedding." He dropped his chin. "You shouldn't lose something you've dreamed of because of me."

"We don't need a wedding, sweetheart. We can go to the courthouse and get married. It's not that important to me." She brought his chin up. "You make me so very happy, Dhruv. You are the kindest, gentlest, most caring partner I could ever hope for. I know I'd be happy for the rest of my life with you."

Dhruv began nodding. "If you're sure."

"I'm positive."

"Okay, then. I'll get a ring and then I'll propose."

Stephanie stifled a chuckle. "I love you, Dhruv."

He sat taller, focused on the new subject of discussion. "What kind of ring do you want?"

"Not diamonds, that's for sure. I was never crazy about them before I lost my sight, and I don't like the angular feel of faceted gems. I'm not sure what I'd want. A gold band is fine."

"You should have an engagement ring. I have an idea."

"I like that."

"I'll surprise you."

"I can't wait!"

She leaned toward him as he reached for her and pulled her against him. Their lips met, and they kissed, long and slow. When they parted, Dhruv slowly got to his feet.

"We've got a lot to decide, but this is enough for now."

"I agree. We've both got work tomorrow. We're in no rush on any of this."

"I love you," he said. "It feels so good to say that."

"I love you, too. And don't give another thought to a wedding, Dhruv. It's not important."

Dhruv stood silently for several moments, then nodded and headed for the door.

CHAPTER 21

*E*mily commanded Garth to find Dhruv's office on Friday afternoon. "Sounds like you're going somewhere," she said once Garth had delivered them to their destination. Dhruv was shutting down his computer.

"I'm leaving early." Dhruv continued to shuffle his papers. "Is that all right?"

"Of course it is," Emily said. "No one on the team puts in more hours than you."

"Did you need something?" Dhruv asked.

"I wanted to tell you I'm going to Denver on Monday."

Dhruv stopped tidying his desk and sat back in his chair. "Why?"

"Howard Kent was very interested in the memo I sent. Your memo. He's invited me to talk to the cybersecurity group."

"Wow! That was fast."

"I know. I just got an email from him and came directly here to tell you. I knew you'd be pleased."

"We should tell the rest of our team."

Emily held up a hand in a stop sign position. "Not yet. I'll know more next week. We don't want to jump the gun."

"If you say so." He picked up his insulated lunch sack and stood. "What will Zoe do when you're gone?"

"My mom will come into the city to stay with her."

"Tell Martha to call me if she needs anything."

"That's nice of you. What are you up to this weekend?"

"I'm going to a jewelry store. That's why I'm leaving early."

"Are you shopping for Stephanie?" Emily asked.

"Yes." Dhruv bit his lower lip. "For her birthday."

"What a great idea. I'm sure she'll love it. You're getting a jump on her gift early. It's not for another couple of months."

"I like to be prepared."

"Are you having a party for her? This will be a landmark birthday—she's turning thirty-five."

"I don't know how to throw parties." He cleared his throat.

"Why don't Zoe and I throw her a party? Oh... we can make it a surprise party." Emily clapped her hands together. "We had so much fun doing Gina's bridal shower. We're pretty good at it, too, aren't we, Garth?" She reached down and rubbed the spot between his ears that he loved.

Dhruv stood still, deep in thought.

"We could invite Martha and your mom and dad. Maybe your uncle, since he owns the building we live in. Her parents, of course. We'll keep it small. I don't think she'd want a big crowd."

Dhruv shifted his weight from foot to foot, thinking.

"Her actual birthday falls on a Saturday. We could get everyone to my apartment by four and you and Stephanie could arrive at four thirty. We'll come up with a plausible-sounding reason for you to come by. Then we'll have a buffet supper. Maybe Mexican? That's her favorite. We've got time to work out the details." She stopped talking and waited for his response.

"Well? What do you think?"

"I think it's a wonderful idea!"

"Do you like it being a surprise?"

"I think a surprise is exactly what we need."

"Great! I'll send out emails this weekend to the people we talked about so they don't make other plans. We'll figure out the rest when I get back from Denver."

"Thank you, Emily."

"I'm so excited about this! Wait until I tell Zoe. She'll be over the moon."

"Can she keep a secret?"

"She most certainly can. I'm more worried about you letting it slip out."

"I'm committed to making it a complete surprise," Dhruv said.

"Then we've got a plan. I'd better go back to my office and let you get to the jeweler."

Dhruv walked with Emily toward her office before peeling off to the elevator bank.

"What do you plan to get her?" Emily called after him.

"I'm going to let that be a surprise for you, too." Dhruv stepped into the elevator, a smile spreading slowly across his lips.

DHRUV HOVERED at the end of the long glass jewelry case that housed wedding bands and diamond engagement rings, shifting his weight from foot to foot.

"Can I help you?" A tiny woman with clear blue eyes and wispy gray hair pulled neatly into a chignon looked up at him. She smiled encouragingly. "An engagement ring, perhaps?" She gestured to the display case between them.

Dhruv nodded. "But not a diamond."

"A sapphire, perhaps? They're very popular."

"No."

"We have some lovely pearls. They're much more afford-able than..."

"It's not the money. My girlfriend is blind. She doesn't like the feel of faceted stones."

"Oh... I see." She pursed her lips, thinking. "Pearls feel wonderful to the touch. Come with me," she motioned for him to follow her to a case on the other side of the room. "We've got several to choose from over here. We can also order a ring for you from our supplier's catalog."

"I want to take it with me now."

Dhruv bent over the case, looking at the pearl rings.

"Let me put the trays on top of the case. You can touch

the rings to see how they'll feel to her." She pulled three trays out of the case and set them in front of Dhruv.

He examined each one with his fingers.

"What do you think?" the woman asked.

"The ones with a single big pearl seem too bulky to me. I don't like the ones with a bunch of small pearls. They're too round—and too fussy."

"Can you describe what you would like?"

"I think it should be an oval. Pearls are round, so I guess that won't work."

The woman tapped his hand. "I think I've got just the thing. It's in the safe. We've had it for years. Wait right here— I'll go get it."

The woman soon returned and handed Dhruv an exquisite ring. A large, oval-shaped opal sat in a plain gold setting.

Dhruv ran his thumb back and forth over the highly polished stone. "It feels nice," he said.

"That's an exceptionally fine stone," the woman said. "It's full of color and life. Opals went out of style for a while. I've always loved this ring. We never put it in our clearance case because it's such a fine piece—we decided to hang onto it until the right buyer came along."

Dhruv cut his eyes from the ring and looked at her.

"It looks like we may have found the perfect owner of this ring," she said.

"Yes. This is it. How much is it?"

The woman took the ring back from him and peered at the tiny tag tied to it. "It'll be eighty percent off of the price on this tag." She held the tag out to him. "It's suddenly on clearance."

"Really?"

"Yes, really." Her voice wavered as she continued. "It makes me so happy that this beautiful ring, which has languished so long in our safe, will now be out in the world as an engagement ring."

"Thank you!"

"What ring size is your girlfriend?"

Dhruv stopped staring at the ring and turned wide eyes to the woman. "Ring size?"

"Yes."

"I don't know."

"Rings have to fit perfectly so they don't fall off. We don't want her to lose it."

"No!"

"After you propose, why don't the two of you come to see me? I can make sure that it fits properly. Will you be buying wedding bands?"

"I don't know. We haven't talked about it."

The woman smiled at the slightly awkward man in front of her—the one who had so thoughtfully picked out a ring for the woman he loved. "We can help you select wedding rings when you bring this in to be sized."

"How long does all this take?"

"Just a few days."

"Good. We'll come in tomorrow morning."

The woman took a step back. "You're planning to propose tonight and you're just shopping for the ring now?"

Dhruv nodded. "I've got the perfect ring, so now I need to go ask her." His voice was matter-of-fact, as if nothing could be more logical.

The woman could barely suppress her chuckle. "I'd better put this in a velvet box so you can be on your way."

"Great. We always watch the PBS NewsHour while we eat. I'll propose right after that."

She hurried away, grinning. She'd seen thousands of men in love over her forty years in the jewelry business. She was certain he would be a steadfast, devoted, and loving husband.

CHAPTER 22

The final strains of the PBS NewsHour theme song began to play on the television in the living room. Dhruv jumped up from his seat at the dining room table and picked up Stephanie's plate, placing it on top of his own. He scooped up the silverware and their glasses with the efficiency of an experienced restaurant server, eager to turn the table for his next customer.

"Let me help," Stephanie said.

"I've got this," he said. "Go into the living room and I'll be right there."

"Okay. Thank you." She walked to the sofa and curled up in a corner, pulling a knit throw over her legs.

Outside, the rain that had been predicted for earlier in the day had finally arrived and drummed against the windows. Biscuit, Sugar, and Rocco lay in a companionable heap by the fireplace.

The sound of running water and dishes clanking together emanated from the kitchen.

"Are you sure you don't need a hand?"

The dishwasher door closed with a thwack and Dhruv was soon at her side.

Stephanie reached over and patted his knee. "You're all keyed up," she said. "I could tell by the way you raced through cleaning up the dishes. You've been in overdrive ever since you got home. What's up?"

"I have something I can't wait to give you."

"You should have said," Stephanie squealed. "We didn't have to watch the news."

"We always watch it. I like to do things in order."

"Of course you do. I know that about you." She leaned toward him. "So... what is it?"

Dhruv took a deep breath, then slid off the edge of the sofa onto his knees, bumping the coffee table as he did so. The stack of books and the remote control that lived on the table clattered to the floor.

"Oh..." Stephanie lunged forward to grab them.

Dhruv caught her in his arms. "Leave that. I'll get it later." He took both of her hands in his.

"Stephanie Wolf—I love you with all my heart. You are the kindest, most compassionate, and funniest person I've ever met. I wish you could see how beautiful you are, too." He took a deep breath. "If you marry me, I'll love you and care for you the rest of my life." He cleared his throat before continuing in a voice thick with emotion. "Will you marry me?"

"Oh, Dhruv…" she began before he interrupted.

"Wait," he said, leaning back and fishing in the pocket of his jeans. "I almost forgot." He pulled and tugged, finally producing a small velvet ring box. He flipped the lid open and pushed it into her hand. "Okay—here's the ring. Now you can talk."

"You got me a ring? That was fast."

"You need a ring to get engaged and I want to be engaged."

Stephanie's fingers traveled over the rigid velvet case to the soft pillow with a slit in the middle that cushioned the ring. "I love velvet," she murmured as she plucked the ring out of the box.

She explored the large oval stone carefully. "This is the wrong shape to be a pearl," she said, bringing the ring to her teeth and running the stone against them. "Nope—this surface is smooth. It's not a pearl."

Dhruv hovered close. "It's an opal. The jeweler said it's a very fine opal."

Stephanie's thumb ran back and forth over the surface. "I love the way it feels. What does it look like?"

"The setting is antique gold. It's bright turquoise with shades of deep blue and has orangey red in the middle. You wear turquoise a lot and you look beautiful."

"It sounds exquisite."

"Try it on."

Stephanie slipped the ring on the appropriate finger of her left hand. The band twirled freely on her finger.

"It's too big," Dhruv stated knowingly. "We need to have it sized."

"Yes. I hate to take it off, but I'd lose it if I tried to wear it like this."

"We can go to the jeweler tomorrow to have it sized."

"I'd love that."

"We can also pick out our wedding rings while we're there."

"Okay, but what's the rush?"

"I think we should get married on your birthday."

Stephanie inhaled slowly. "That's an idea. Then you'll never forget our anniversary," she teased.

"I won't ever forget," he stated matter-of-factly. "Emily is throwing you a surprise birthday party."

"That's nice of her." Stephanie chuckled. "I'm glad you told me. I hate surprises."

"We can still have a surprise. It's just that it will be a surprise for them, not you." Dhruv laid out his plan.

"That's a genius idea, Dhruv. I've been thinking that both our parents would be terribly disappointed if we went off and got married. They need to be there. And we both want Emily and Zoe."

"Plus Martha."

"For sure. She's such a dear."

"Who will perform the ceremony?"

"My coworker, Rhonda, can perform marriages in California. She's wonderful. I could ask her."

"That's fine with me."

"We'll have to go to the county clerk to get our license."

"I've got a half day on Tuesday. Could you take off work so we can go then?"

"Yep."

"It's all set, then," Stephanie said slowly, her mind spinning over any overlooked details. "Let's not tell anyone we're engaged. We can save the rings for the ceremony. That way, we'll avoid all the questions from our families about what we intend to do for our wedding."

"That's a great idea."

"I don't want anyone to come up with ideas or suggestions that we have to dodge or reject. This way, no one will get their feelings hurt."

"Brilliant."

"Now I've got to figure out what to wear."

"Velvet," Dhruv said. "You just said you love velvet."

"That's a great idea. I'll order several dresses online. You can help me choose which one to keep."

"No. That'd be bad luck."

"For someone who doesn't like weddings, you sure know all the folklore surrounding them."

"I research."

"We've got a plan, then. I'll soon be thirty-five and a married lady."

"There's one more thing. A very important thing."

"What's that?"

"You never answered. Will you marry me?"

Stephanie threw her arms around his neck and pulled him to her. "Yes," she whispered before she lost herself in his kiss.

CHAPTER 23

$\mathcal{I}$ poked my nose through the gap between the front seats and rested my muzzle on the console. We were in Grant's car. Unlike the last time we'd ridden with him, Emily wasn't relaxed and happy. She wasn't unhappy, mind you. Her energy was more like one part anticipation and three parts anxiety.

"You're going to be fine," Grant said, reaching over me to squeeze Emily's hand. "You and Garth have got this, haven't you, boy?"

I lifted my eyes to his. Of course we did. I had no idea what we were going to do, but it didn't matter. Emily and I were trained for anything and everything.

"I'm glad I'm going to Denver to pitch Dhruv's cyberattack proposal, but I haven't flown since I came back from my honeymoon—when my retinas detached." Emily said. "I'm nervous."

"That must have been pure hell," Grant said. "This time is different."

"I've been going over my checklist in my mind," Emily said. "My boarding pass is on my phone. I submitted the US Department of Transportation Service Animal Air Transportation Form online. A copy of it and the approval email I got back from them with Garth's Service Animal ID number are in my carry-on bag. The flight is less than three hours and Garth won't need to relieve himself, so I don't need the Service Animal Relief Attestation Form."

"Sounds like Garth is all set."

"He should be. I have my passport for identification to get through security, my laptop is in the outside pouch of my carry-on, and I'm not spending the night, so I don't have any toiletries. I've got a trusted traveler number, so I don't have to take off my shoes or jacket, and my laptop can stay put."

"I was hoping you had TSA PreCheck. All you'll have to pull out for the X-ray machine is your phone and your watch."

Emily patted the side of her purse. "My cane is folded in here." She collapsed against the back of her seat.

"You said that the airport will have someone assist you from curbside check-in to security. The TSA will have a passenger support specialist accompany you through security, and then the airport assistant will see you to your gate."

"That's the plan."

"I'm happy to park and escort you to security myself."

"I know you are—and I appreciate it—but I need to learn

to do this on my own." Emily lifted her hair off the nape of her neck and sucked in a ragged breath.

Grant glanced at her. "You're hot?" He lowered the temperature on his car's air conditioner.

Emily shook her head.

"You've made all the necessary arrangements. You'll be fine."

"I know. I'm..." she paused, then continued, "I'm a nervous flier. Always have been. Once the plane takes off, I'm fine. Until we start our descent for landing. I know it's irrational. I've tried breathing techniques and listening to music —nothing helps."

"I've found that writing my name over and over—with my left hand—does the trick."

"Really? You don't like to fly, either?"

"It's not my favorite thing to do, but this writing thing helps me. There's science behind writing with your nondominant hand."

"Interesting." Emily leaned forward, moving her left hand against her knee in a writing motion. "I'll try it."

"You've got another tool in your arsenal that you've never had before." He rested his hand on top of my muzzle.

I swung my tail, thumping the back of her seat.

"Garth! Of course. I'll be fine if Garth's with me."

I thumped my tail harder.

Grant pulled his car to the curbside check-in for our airline. He jumped out of the car and pulled Emily's carry-on out of his trunk while Emily and I got out.

An attendant greeted Emily by name and said they'd been expecting her.

Emily's hand on my harness telegraphed less anxiety than when we'd said goodbye to Zoe and Martha outside our apartment earlier that morning.

Grant leaned in and kissed Emily goodbye. "Have a great trip. I'll pick you up tonight when you get back."

"It'll be almost nine. We can take a cab or rideshare home."

"Nonsense. I've already arranged for Mom to stay with Diedre. I'll want to hear all about your presentation on the way home. Go knock their socks off."

"Ma'am." The airport assistant cleared his throat.

"You're the best, Grant," Emily said. I could hear she was smiling.

"Take good care of her, boy," Grant called after us as Emily commanded me to follow the airport man.

I stepped out at a brisk pace, through a double set of automatic glass doors, into the chaotic scene of a busy airport on a Monday morning. I ignored all the exclamations and admiring glances directed to me, and focused on following the man. Taking good care of Emily was my mission in life.

THE TSA HELPER WAS SUPER. We followed her to the head of a long line of people. No one complained. She helped Emily put her purse and carry-on bag through the X-ray machine, together with a dish that held Emily's watch and phone.

Our next stop was the full-body scanning machine. I wasn't sure how we would handle this, but Emily knew.

She told me to sit and stay at the entrance to the machine. Emily then went into the machine, holding my leash. The lady helped her put her feet and hands in the right place. The machine whooshed but didn't buzz.

Emily stepped to the other side of the machine and commanded me to come.

I walked through the scanner and the nice TSA lady ran a stick that she called a wand over my harness. When she was done with that, she ran her hands around and under my collar, spending extra time on the area between my ears. My collar wasn't anywhere near there. Her hands felt fantastic. She was an A-plus ear-rubber in my book. I wagged my tail in response—I was pretty sure this wasn't a TSA-required maneuver.

She called me a very good boy and made sure we collected all of our items from the conveyor before taking us to the airport assistant who took us to our gate.

Emily sat on a chair bolted to the floor in a long line of chairs. She took out the braille copy of her notes and began re-reading her presentation.

The airport was full of interesting smells and people. I settled at her feet, but kept my eyes on our surroundings.

A crackly voice finally sounded on a loudspeaker close by. Emily hurriedly stuffed her notes into her purse, pulled her phone with her boarding pass from the compartment where she'd carefully stowed it, and commanded me to find the desk.

I jumped to my feet. I was ready to get going onto the next thing—whatever that would be.

Emily showed her boarding pass and my papers to the man behind the desk.

He glanced at them, then directed us to follow him. We walked through a tunnel to an oddly shaped metal door.

The man told Emily to step up onto the plane.

We did, and he led us to our seat toward the front of the plane.

Emily slid across the row to the window seat. She positioned me with my back under the seat in front of her and my face pointing toward her shoes.

The man asked Emily if she needed anything out of her bag, then told her he was putting it into the bin above our heads.

I had every intention of staying awake to see who else would be getting on our plane. Would there be any other dogs like me? I lay my head down on Emily's shoes—for only a second. The next thing I knew, Emily's hand was on the top of my head and she was calling my name.

"We're in Denver, Garth. We made it!"

I pushed myself to my feet and stretched as much as I could in the cramped space.

"I'm ready, Garth. I'm going to do well."

CHAPTER 24

*T*he airport assistant met Emily at the gate.

"I hope you had a good flight," the man said.

"Very smooth," Emily said, realizing with a start that she hadn't experienced the panic attacks she usually had when flying. She had forgotten about writing her name with her left hand. Grant had been right—Garth's presence had distracted and calmed her.

"Could you lead us to the animal relief area before taking us to the rideshare line?"

"Of course. I was about to ask if this guy needed a break. It's not far."

The assistant walked on, and Emily and Garth followed. He opened a door and allowed them to enter. "You're the only ones here. There's a patch of turf and a fake rock."

"Good. This guy loves rocks."

"There are disposable bags and a hand washing sink on the wall on your right."

"Excellent." Emily and Garth entered the small room. "Garth, let's do your business."

Garth made a beeline for the rock and relieved himself. He then moved away from it and hunched to complete his task.

Emily ran her hand over his back, confirming from his posture that she needed a disposal bag. She placed her foot near the base of Garth's tail to mark the spot and pulled a plastic dog waste bag from a small roll in her purse.

Garth stood and returned to her side.

Emily placed the bag over her hand, using it like a glove, and located and scooped up his recent deposit.

The assistant guided her to the waste can and the sink. They were soon on their way to the rideshare line.

Emily's shoulders relaxed. Everything was going according to plan.

"Rideshares will arrive on your left side," the assistant said.

"I can hear that's where cars are coming from," Emily said. "How many people are here? It sounds busy."

"There are eight people here, other than you. It's always busy on Monday mornings. Is there anything else you need? I'll stay with you until your ride arrives."

"That's not necessary," Emily said. "I've got it from here." She handed the man a generous tip and thanked him for his help.

Emily pulled her phone from her purse, dictated quick

texts to her mom and Grant that she had arrived in Denver, then opened her rideshare app and ordered a car.

The screen reader told her the car would be there in under two minutes, giving her the name and number of the driver.

She commanded Garth to take her to the curb, where she listened closely for her name. She didn't have long to wait.

A male voice called to her from a spot to her left.

She raised her free hand over her head and swung it back and forth as she called "here." Emily commanded Garth to move forward.

"You're Emily?"

"Yes. And you are?"

The man gave her his name, and it matched the one that the app had given her as her driver.

"I'm headed downtown," Emily said, expecting the man to open the car door for her and Garth.

"I'll take you," the man said, "but not your dog."

"He's a service dog."

"I don't care what he is. I'm allergic to dogs."

"I'm blind, sir, and Garth is my guide dog. By law, you have to allow him to come with me."

"I don't think so."

Emily pulled her shoulders back and opened the rideshare app on her phone. "Let's call customer service. They'll confirm what I'm telling you." She listened as she punched her way through a long series of recorded menu options, never reaching a human being or a recording with the information she was seeking.

"This is my car and I don't have to do anything I don't want to."

Emily's face grew warm, and she took a deep, calming breath. "Look—I'm sorry you're allergic to dogs. Garth is extremely well groomed. He had a bath this weekend. I don't think he has enough dander to bother you—and we can keep the windows open, if you'd like."

"Sorry, lady."

"But you can't refuse to take us," Emily said, her voice cracking with emotion.

"Find yourself another ride." The man's voice trailed off as he walked to the driver's side. He got into his vehicle and drove off.

Emily stood on the sidewalk, blinking hard, as people on either side moved past her, on their way from the terminal to their waiting car.

She swallowed hard and shook her head. Standing here, in tears, was not moving her closer to her destination. She swiped under her eyes with her thumb. If she hurried, she could still make it to her meeting on time. She took a deep breath and requested another ride. She'd file a complaint later against the noncompliant driver who had just abandoned her. What she needed to do now was get herself—and Garth—to that meeting.

CHAPTER 25

*H*oward Kent, EVP of Systems and Programs, greeted Emily warmly as she was ushered into the largest conference room at her company's regional headquarters in Denver. "Here's the person we've all been waiting to meet," he said, moving to her and taking her right hand in his to shake it.

"I'm sorry I'm late," Emily replied. "I had a bit of an issue with my rideshare."

"No worries. Travel is always uncertain," Howard said. "The main thing is, you're here now." He led her to a seat at the end of a long table and held out the chair for her.

Emily felt for the arms of the chair and sat down, placing her purse over the back of the chair and her carry-on bag on the tabletop. Garth settled at her feet.

Howard stood next to her chair and addressed the room. "Everyone, this is Emily Main. She runs the most successful programming group in the company. You may remember the disastrous issue we had last year with an operating system update—things got so bad that our stock price plummeted. Her team found the problem and fixed it—even though it wasn't in their area of responsibility."

Howard paused, but no one spoke. Emily heard a room full of people breathing in and out. She couldn't tell how many were in attendance.

"One of Emily's very talented team members has written a memo identifying a security risk and outlining a program he thinks could be developed to address it. Since this is your area of expertise, I thought you might want to collaborate with Emily's team. I know that you've all been working overtime to address the wide variety of issues on your plate. Tapping into resources from another division should be very welcome."

He stopped talking and was again met with stony silence.

Emily lifted her chin and faced the darkness before her. *Should she begin?*

Howard answered that question.

"I'd planned to stay with you all, but I have to step out. Emily will take the floor—she's prepared a presentation explaining her team's proposal—but first, I'd like you to go around the room and introduce yourselves to Emily." He turned and spoke to her. "I'll be in touch with you later in the week."

"Thank you," she replied, hoping she sounded more confident than she felt.

"Ross Wilcox is the director of this unit. I'll turn it over to you, Ross. I trust that you'll give Emily anything she needs while she's here."

"Of course," came a booming voice from the other end of the table. "We've got a nice afternoon planned for her." Ross stood as Howard left the room. "I've been director of the cybersecurity unit since it was founded in the early 2000s. We've been working on these issues since before you were out of high school, Emily." His voice was ripe with false sincerity. "Let's go around the room..."

Emily listened carefully and took notes as the people, twenty-four of them as it turned out, seated with her at the table introduced themselves. They all had impressive educational backgrounds and robust industry experience. The newest addition to their team had joined them more than five years earlier.

Emily pursed her lips. She was about to address a close-knit group of professionals about an issue that was squarely within their area of expertise—and she was going to tell them why her team could handle the issue better and more efficiently.

"That's all of us," Ross said. "Howard assembled us to hear from you, Emily. How can we do things better?"

Emily winced.

Chairs creaked and groaned as everyone turned toward her.

"I've got a short PowerPoint presentation to share with you," Emily said, tugging at the zipper on her carry-on that was now suddenly stuck. "Can someone lower a screen and help me hook up my laptop?" She continued to yank the zipper, which finally gave way.

A person on her right whose first name she remembered was Kari got out of her seat and helped Emily connect her laptop to a large white screen that hung on the wall behind Emily.

"Thank you," Emily said, laying out her braille notes flat on the table next to her laptop. "First, let me return the favor by introducing my team members." She ran through each name, providing educational distinctions and significant achievements of each one from memory. "Like your team, we've been working together for many years. As Howard indicated, Dhruv has planned an approach to a very serious security risk. If you'll turn your attention to the screen, my first slide outlines the risk…"

Emily proceeded with her forty-minute presentation, working through her slides with growing confidence. Her screen reader identified the slide number on the screen and, after the third slide, she didn't need to refer to her braille notes.

"This is a brief overview of a proposed response to a very complex problem," Emily said as she concluded her presentation. "I'm sure you have a lot of questions." She paused and waited.

The responsive silence was thundering.

"Anyone?" Emily spoke into the darkness in front of her.

Again, no one spoke.

Emily closed her laptop.

"Thank you for coming, Emily." Ross leapt out of his seat. "Let's give her a round of applause, everyone."

A smattering of applause went around the room.

Emily felt her pulse throb in her temples. They were patronizing her. The only reason she was here was because Howard had arranged it. But Ross's division didn't report to Howard, and they had no intention of taking her seriously. For all she knew, no one had paid attention to a word she'd said. They'd probably been checking their emails on their phones the whole time.

"Kari's our newest addition to our team," Ross said. "She'll give you a tour of the regional headquarters and take you to lunch before you head back to the airport. Now, I think we've all got important things to attend to..."

"You think this is a joke, don't you?" Emily recognized her own voice and wondered what in the world she was doing.

"I'm sorry?" Ross replied, sounding taken aback.

"If you even listened to my presentation, you're not taking it seriously."

"We've been successfully managing the company's cyber-security risks for years." Ross's voice took a nasty tone. "We know what we're doing and we definitely don't need advice from outsiders."

Emily responded to his words like a bull to a red flag. "Then what are you doing to address the risk we identified? As far as my team could tell, you're ignoring it," she replied with steely resolve.

The room grew even more quiet, as if everyone was holding their breath.

"Rest. Assured. We. Are. Doing. Everything. We. Need. To. Do."

"I hope you are. I'm afraid time will tell." Emily jammed her laptop into her carry-on and scooped up her notes. "Now—if Kari is still available to give me that tour—I'd love it."

She stood, slung her purse and carry-on bag over her shoulder, and grabbed Garth's harness.

"Right this way," Kari said, leading them out of the room. Emily had no way of knowing that the eyes that followed her exit were full of equal parts amazement, irritation, and— with the exception of Ross's—admiration.

CHAPTER 26

"We have ten full floors in this building," Kari said while they waited for the elevator. "Marketing takes up four of them. They're a much livelier bunch than we are."

Emily forced a smile as she tried to fix her attention on Kari, but wound up replaying her heated exchange with Ross in her mind. He was an arrogant ass, defending his turf. The more she thought about it, the more convinced she was that he wasn't taking the threat her team had identified seriously.

The elevator chimed, and Kari held the door open for Emily and Garth. She pushed the button, the doors closed, and the elevator began to climb.

"We're the only ones in here?" Emily asked.

"Yes."

"You don't have to answer this—I realize it's unfair of me

to ask—but your group isn't working on anything to address the risk I talked about, is it?"

Kari cleared her throat. "No."

The elevator arrived at its floor.

The back of Emily's neck prickled with her irritation. "You know what? You don't need to give me a tour. I won't take up any more of your time. Garth and I can head back to the airport."

The three of them stayed in the elevator.

"Let's get out of here," Kari replied, and pushed the button for the lobby. "For what it's worth, I agree with you. I've been saying the same thing for months. It's like I'm talking, but no one hears me."

The elevator stopped on the first floor. The three of them stepped out.

"I know the perfect spot to take us for lunch," Kari said. "It's on the way to the airport. I'll drop you off when we're done."

"Are you sure you can be gone that long? I thought we'd grab a bite somewhere near here. I can take a cab or rideshare to the airport."

"I'd like to talk to you," Kari said. "About your presentation. I know a few of the others in that room are interested, too."

"You could have fooled me. Why didn't anyone ask questions or make a comment?"

"That's what I'd like to talk about," Kari said. "I have time. Ross expects me to babysit..." she stopped suddenly and cleared her throat, "I mean, spend the afternoon with you."

"If you're sure."

"My car's in the garage. There's a separate bank of elevators. Follow me."

"TELL ME ABOUT THIS PLACE," Emily said as they were shown to their table. She pulled a chair with a curved iron back away from a small round table topped with a cotton tablecloth and sat. "It smells sweet—like baked goods—and sort of clean and fresh."

Kari chuckled. "That's an accurate description. We're at a little tea room near my house. You're smelling their freshly baked scone-of-the-day. The menu board says it's lemon blueberry."

"That sounds yummy."

"They also have the best salads in town. All the ingredients are organic—sourced from local farms."

"Do you have a favorite?"

"They're all great, but I always end up ordering the chopped kale with grapefruit, free range chicken, and pine nuts."

"Let's order two of those salads—and scones," Emily said. "Lunch will be on my expense account."

"I won't argue with that."

The server took their orders and brought them each a tall glass of elderberry iced tea. "Can I give this guy some water?"

"Thank you," Emily said. "That's very thoughtful of you."

The server moved off and Kari began. "I brought you to

this place because no one from work ever comes here. I don't want to be overheard."

"That sounds a bit..."

"Paranoid?" Kari completed Emily's sentence. "I guess I am." She rested her elbows on the table and raked her fingers through her hair. "Let me give you some background. Ross was my supervisor when I started here. He was competent technically and was decent to work for."

"Was?"

"Exactly. He got a promotion six months after I started, and he moved into the director position a year later."

"He's a fast-tracker."

"Yes." Kari leaned over the table and, although they were not near anyone who could overhear, she lowered her voice. "This won't go any farther?"

"Of course not. Unless you think he's done something that violates the corporate code of ethics," Emily added perfunctorily.

Kari remained still, as if frozen in place.

The server bent down to put a bowl of water on the floor next to Garth, who noisily quenched his thirst. "I'll be right back with your salads."

"Oh, my God! You think he's committed a violation?"

"No. Not really." Kari twisted her hands together, over and over. "It's just that he's so controlling of all of us. He knows everything we're working on in minute detail."

The server set their salads in front of them. He placed a basket of scones, wrapped in an embroidered linen napkin, between them. "Enjoy."

"Those smell amazing," Emily said. "The lemon is unmistakable."

Kari opened the napkin. "Help yourself. There's a bread plate to the left of your fork." Kari removed a small dish containing pats of butter molded into the shape of a flower. "Can I put a pat of butter on your plate?"

"I'll never say no to butter." Emily placed a pat onto the warm scone and took a generous bite, the melting butter running down her fingers. She wiped them on her napkin, then continued. "In all fairness, my employees might say the same about me."

"It's not just that. In our area of responsibility, we're supposed to keep our eyes open for anything out of the ordinary."

"I would think so."

"Ross never wants to hear about things we think might be a problem. He dismisses our ideas and belittles our efforts." Her words came faster. "He's mean about it, too. Demeaning. Nasty."

"Maybe he's one of those people who doesn't know how to be a manager. He'd function better as a worker bee." Emily dug into her salad.

"I've wondered about that. I've also thought he won't listen to me because I'm a woman. You noticed that I'm the only one in the department?"

"I did. That thought occurred to me when I was," she paused, selecting her words, "discussing my presentation with him."

"I loved that 'discussion.' It was gratifying to see someone stand up to him. I know the rest of our team thought so, too. I'm sure they'll be talking about it all afternoon."

Emily gave a wan smile. "You were saying you feel discounted because you're a woman?"

Kari paused with her fork in midair. "It's so frustrating. I can make a suggestion in a meeting and no one reacts. Two minutes later, one of the guys proposes the same thing I just did, and everyone thinks it's a genius idea."

"Every working woman has had that experience."

"It sucks."

"It certainly does. The main thing is to not let it get under your skin. Don't allow that treatment to strip you of your self-confidence."

"Easier said than done. It's so insipid—it's challenging to guard against it."

"I agree."

"Anyway—whatever we're working on has to come from him."

Emily sat, silently considering this.

"It's not right, Emily. We're supposed to be a team of watchdogs for the company. A group of us approached him nine months ago about the risk you just talked to us about. We didn't have the solution you proposed—or any solution, for that matter. We wanted to work on one."

"He said 'no'?"

"He said that we were worried about things that hadn't happened to anyone in our industry. He said we've got systems in place that will protect the company. But he was angry with us for bringing it up. The answer wasn't just 'no,' but 'hell no.' " She took a sip of her tea. "He berated us and then loaded so much additional work on us—on a project with a very low level of exposure—that no one had time to think twice."

"That is odd," Emily said. "Why do you think he did that?"

"Ego. As you can see, he has no shortage of that. It wasn't his idea, so it couldn't be a good one." Kari speared a forkful of her salad. "The four of us who approached Ross earlier were getting so excited during your presentation. You couldn't see us, but we were sending text messages to each other, saying that your team had raised the problem we'd identified—and come up with a plan to solve it."

"Then why didn't you speak up?"

"You couldn't see Ross's face. If looks could kill, Emily." Kari paused. "We knew he was seething about your even being there. Maybe I shouldn't say this, but he told us that morning that Howard was doing a dog-and-pony show for a diversity hire and we were to listen to the presentation and ask no questions so we could get back to work as soon as possible."

"What?! He was patronizing me because I'm blind? That little shit!" Emily tossed her fork onto her plate in disgust.

"I shouldn't have told you that. I'm sorry. That was hurtful."

"It is, but I need to know. I'm glad you told me." Emily took a long sip from her iced tea. "I could report him to HR."

"If you do, he'll know I told you. He's so vindictive," Kari said, panic rising in her voice. She took an audible breath. "I'm sorry I said that. He's a pig. I should report him myself."

"Let's keep our powder dry on all this," Emily said, drawing out the words as she thought. "I don't think either of us needs to do anything about this."

"Ross can't do anything to impact your career. And Howard Kent is on your side. He's at the top of the food chain. Plus, rumor has it that your team loves you. Everyone wants to work for you."

"Thank you, Kari. No offense, but I've got the best team in the company." Emily checked the time on her watch. "Let's finish our lunch. I'd like to be at the airport early. I want to make sure Garth has plenty of time to visit the animal relief area and I can catch up on my email."

"I'll get the server to bring our check," Kari said.

"If you ever get tired of working for Ross and would be interested in moving to San Francisco, call me. I think you'd be a perfect fit for my team. I'd have to clear it with Ross first, of course."

The smile that erupted on Kari's face eradicated the tension that had accompanied their discussion. "Thank you, Emily. I've got family responsibilities that keep me in Denver, but this means the world to me."

"I understand. If things change for you, let me know. The offer stands."

Emily paid the check, and the three of them headed for the airport.

CHAPTER 27

"We've been stopped for a while now." Emily tried to push down her rising anxiety.

"My GPS shows an accident up ahead. They're merging all the traffic into one lane."

"Any idea how long we'll be delayed? I should be at the airport by now."

"Maybe another twenty minutes? I'm so sorry."

"Can you get off the freeway and take surface streets?"

"Not really. Slogging through this is our best bet. We'll be cutting it close, but I think you'll make your flight."

Emily unbuttoned her blazer and pulled the collar away from her neck.

"Do you have anyone who helps you at the airport?"

"Yes. They were terrific in San Francisco this morning. I'll see if I can alert the airline that I'm going to be much later getting there than I thought."

"Good idea."

Emily opened the airline's app on her phone and followed the screen reader's prompts to navigate to the appropriate page. "There—I've updated my arrival time to the airport." She checked her flight's status and learned it was delayed by thirty minutes. "That should help."

"We're just about to clear the accident," Kari said. "The GPS shows traffic is running normally as soon as we get past it. We should be curbside in another fifteen minutes."

Emily pulled her purse onto her lap and unzipped the pouch with her travel papers. She confirmed that she had everything she needed, then retrieved two folded twenty-dollar bills from her wallet and slipped them into her pocket. She was more than willing to generously tip the assistants who would help her make her flight.

"I can come in with you, if you'd like," Kari said as she accelerated to highway speeds.

"I think it'll be faster if you drop me off curbside. An airport employee will meet me there and give me all the help I'll need."

"If you're sure? This has been a long day for you—I hate to think of your dealing with any snafus."

"I'll be fine," Emily said, wishing she felt confident that she would be. "You've done more than enough for me."

Kari continued to accelerate as she pulled into the left lane and sailed past cars on her right. "The airport exit is two miles ahead," she said.

Emily listened to the time on her phone. "We're going to

make it. Just." She inhaled deeply. "Thank you, Kari. I really want to get home tonight."

Kari turned on her blinker and sailed onto the exit ramp. "We're here." She slowed and pulled to a stop. "This is your airline."

Emily threw her door open, gathered her purse and carry-on, and retrieved Garth from the back seat. "Thank you—for everything," she called as she slammed the door shut.

"Safe trip," Kari called after her, but Emily and Garth were already hurrying to the check-in desk.

I KNEW she was upset in the car. Emily was trying to keep her voice calm when she talked to the nice woman who was driving, but I could tell she was struggling. I took her to the check-in counter as fast as I could.

"What do you mean, the airport assistant left?"

"I'm so sorry, ma'am, but you're too late to make your flight. We thought you weren't coming, and he just left."

"I updated my arrival time on the app and my flight has been delayed. I can still make it, but I'll need help to get through the airport."

The man tapped on his keyboard. "You're right. If we can get you through security, you might be in luck."

"Thank God."

"*If* we can get an assistant," he continued to tap on his

keyboard. "Okay—I've requested immediate help. Please go through the doors to your left and wait inside." He gave her a number. "The assistant will call out that number."

"Thank you," Emily said, her breaths short and jerky. She wasn't happy.

We moved through the doors and stepped to one side. I stood next to her, scanning the crowd. I wasn't sure what we were looking for, but I could tell we were waiting for something important.

"Come on," Emily muttered under her breath, craning her neck to listen for that number.

We continued to wait. She tapped her watch. "We've been here five minutes, where is…" She stopped abruptly and her free hand shot into the air as a male voice called out a series of numbers. "I'm over here."

"Emily Main? I'm so sorry for the delay. I thought—"

"No worries." She cut him off. "My flight is already boarding. Can we make it?"

"If I walk fast, can you follow?"

I rolled my eyes. He'd never seen anyone walk faster than Emily and me.

"Yes!"

The man took off, and I lasered in on him like we were the only living beings in the airport. We made good time to the security checkpoint and the TSA helpers were even more efficient than they'd been in San Francisco. I stayed true to our mission and leaned away from the person who ran his hands under my collar. I know he would have given me a good rub, but we didn't have time.

Our airport assistant met us when we got through security. "You're at the farthest gate, but we'll make it."

"I need to let Garth stop at an animal relief area. And I'd like to go to the ladies' room."

"We'll pass both on the way. Come on."

He took off again, and we kept pace.

"There's a ladies' room up ahead, but there's a long line."

"Don't stop," Emily said.

"The animal relief area is next," he called over his shoulder.

We stopped, and I made short work of my business.

We were soon zipping along behind the man again.

"There's another ladies' up ahead," the man said.

We kept going.

The man slowed down. "There's a line, again."

Emily moaned and sucked in a breath. "I can't miss my flight. I'll wait until I'm on the plane."

The man lengthened his stride, and we trotted to keep up.

He finally stopped at the last gate in the terminal. All the chairs in the seating area were empty. A woman was behind a counter and a man was standing by the door to the tunnel that led to the plane.

"This woman has a ticket on this flight," the man said, his chest heaving.

"We've finished boarding. We're about to close the door."

"There was an accident on the freeway that made her late," the man said. "We've run all the way."

"I'll take it from here." The woman's tone was stern. "Thank you."

Emily placed her phone open to her boarding pass on the counter in front of the woman.

"I've paid for a seat on this plane and I'm here before you've closed the door. Surely you can allow us..."

The woman leaned over the desk to peer at me.

"You're with a dog?"

"My guide dog," Emily said, her tone firm.

"You'll need a ticket for him. We only have one open seat left."

"I do NOT need a ticket for Garth. He can ride at my feet."

The man who had been tidying a stack of papers by the door looked at the brewing argument going on above my head. He hurried over to us.

"This lady and her dog want to get on the plane."

The man looked at me and then Emily. "You're a ticketed passenger?"

"I am." Emily slid her phone toward him.

He examined it and motioned for the woman to step back.

"Right this way. Let me see you to the plane. We're ready to leave as soon as you're situated."

We followed him down the tunnel.

"We're at the door," the man said to Emily. "There's a slight step up."

We entered the plane. "Your steward will see you to your seat."

"Thank you for intervening," Emily said as he disappeared back into the tunnel.

I waited patiently at Emily's side.

Emily showed the steward our boarding pass.

"You're two rows ahead," she said. "The open seat is on the aisle. He can't stick out into the aisle."

"I reserved a window seat."

"Someone's taken it."

"Then make the person in my window seat move to the aisle." Emily's voice was like ice.

The woman moved down the aisle, and I followed.

She addressed the occupant of the window seat. "I know we're ready to leave, but I'm afraid I'm going to have to ask you to move. This woman," she gestured with her head to Emily, "is in the window seat."

"I'm in the window seat," said an overweight man in a rumpled business suit. He pulled a satchel from the seat-back in front of him and rummaged for his ticket, handing it to the steward.

She looked from his paper to Emily's and back again. "It looks like we've double booked this seat."

"You said the aisle seat is empty," Emily said. "I can't legally sit there with my guide dog."

"I'm not moving," the man said. "This is the airline's fault."

A drop of moisture landed on my nose. I looked up. My Emily was crying softly. I pushed my muzzle into her hand and licked it. Whatever was going on, we'd get through it together. I was pretty sure it involved me. I stared at the steward, willing her to notice me. I could sit neatly in the aisle seat. No problem.

Another steward approached from the front of the plane. "What's the problem? We need to get out of the gate."

"We have to find a window seat for them," the steward said. "If you'd have gotten to the airport on time and boarded early—like people with special needs are supposed to—we wouldn't be having this problem."

Emily dug in her pocket for a tissue and swiped it under her eyes.

I was the first one to notice the woman with the thinning gray hair and vibrant blue eyes in the window seat on the other side of the aisle. She put her purse on her arm and began sliding over the two people between her and us. "They can have my seat," she said to the stewards, squeezing her tiny frame over the other passengers.

The stewards moved back to make room for her.

"I don't mind the aisle seat."

I watched as she sank into the open seat.

"Thank you," Emily said.

The other passengers in the row got up and moved into the aisle to allow us to get to our seat.

"I'll have to put your carry-on in the back," said the steward. "All the overhead compartments here are full."

"I've got room for it in front of me," said the elderly lady. "No need to separate her from her bag."

The steward transferred the bag from Emily to the woman as I settled into position and the other passengers regained their seats.

Emily leaned forward and turned her face toward the aisle. "Thank you for being so kind."

"You're welcome," came the reply. "Enjoy the flight."

Emily secured her seat belt and the overhead PA system crackled in a way that hurt my ears. The plane began to move, and we were soon on our way home.

CHAPTER 28

"*T*here's a man with a giant bouquet of flowers waving at you and walking straight toward us," the airport attendant said. "I don't think you'll have to be picked up downstairs."

Emily's drooping shoulders straightened. "I didn't think he'd park and come inside to meet me."

The attendant smiled. He'd seen hundreds of happy airport greetings and he never got tired of them.

"Hello, sweetheart," Grant said, lifting Emily's carry-on off of her shoulder.

"You're good?" the attendant asked.

"I am. Thank you." She reached into her purse for her wallet.

"I've got this," Grant said, handing the man a tip.

"Have a good night," the attendant said as he left them.

"You didn't have to do that," Emily said. Grant put his arms around Emily and pulled her to him.

People brushed by them on both sides.

"We're in everyone's way," Emily murmured against his chest.

"I don't care," Grant said, tilting her chin to his and kissing her.

Emily rested her head on his shoulder when they pulled apart.

"Hard day?"

"You could say that."

"Was it the meeting or the travel?"

"Both."

"Oh, geez. I don't like the sound of that. Have you eaten?"

"I had a late lunch."

They moved toward the parking garage.

"Let's grab food on the way home."

"My flight was late—it's after ten. Don't you have to work tomorrow?"

"I've been known to stay up late on a work night and still be able to function the next day." He rubbed her back as they walked. "I'm thinking comfort food is in order. There are tons of all-night diners."

Emily sighed, releasing the tension she'd been holding in since she'd stepped into regional headquarters. "That sounds lovely, actually."

"We can sit down and you can tell me everything."

"We may be there for hours."

"That's fine by me. My mom is with Diedre. I'm all yours."

"Let me text Mom to tell her I've landed and we're getting something to eat. I don't want her to wait up."

"Do we need to stop somewhere to get food for this guy?" He pointed to Garth.

"I brought his kibble with me. I'd planned to feed him at the airport before we came back, but you wouldn't believe what happened. We almost missed our flight." She launched into the tale of the trials and tribulations of their travel.

"I hate that you went through all that," Grant said as they pulled to the curb in front of a popular diner. "You could report the woman at the counter in Denver."

"I'm going to," Emily said. "The airline needs to make sure their employees know the laws about service animals. To tell you the truth, the worst part was needing to go to the bathroom the entire flight home."

"What?"

"The two passengers next to me were asleep, and I didn't want to wake them so I could get out of my seat. The flight was bumpy and the captain kept us in our seats most of the way, too. Garth and I bolted off that plane when we landed." She reached her hand through the console between the front seats to pat him. "Garth can find the closest restroom anywhere. I'm always in good hands with him."

"Seriously?"

"Yes. And he knows which one is a women's restroom. He never gets it wrong."

"Well done, fella," Grant said. He got out of the car and

came around the front as Emily stepped onto the sidewalk. He opened the back door for Garth and picked up the carry-on containing his kibble and travel bowl.

They entered the diner. Butter-yellow walls and booths upholstered in sparkly red vinyl created a cheerful throw-back to the 1960s.

A woman stood behind the hostess stand, wiping a stack of vinyl menus. "We're not busy. Where would you like to sit?"

"Somewhere quiet," Grant said. "We've got a lot to talk about."

The woman took two menus from her stack. "Follow me."

"I'm planning to feed Garth," Emily said.

"No problem," the woman said. "I'll bring him some water."

"Thank you," Emily said, relief evident in her voice. "How was your day?" Emily asked Grant as they settled into their booth.

"Fine. Busy. All regular stuff."

The server came to their table, bringing water for Garth.

"I know what I want," Emily said. "I'm starving."

"I'm ready," said the server. "What'll you have?"

"A cheeseburger—add bacon, fries, and a chocolate shake."

"Glad to see you're embracing the comfort food theme," Grant said. "I'll have the same."

The server took their menus. "I'll get your shakes right out."

"So—I'm hoping that your problems with your flight were the worst part of your day."

"I'm afraid not."

"I'm all ears."

Emily set a bowl of kibble on the floor for Garth and related the events of her day at regional headquarters, supplying details as Grant asked questions. They worked their way through their juicy burgers and tall stack of fries as she talked.

"What do you think?" Emily asked, pushing her empty plate away from her. "Am I misreading this?"

"No. Of course not. This Wilcox guy didn't want you anywhere near his turf. His response had nothing to do with the quality of your memo or your presentation."

Emily sighed heavily.

"Don't let him get in your head, Em. You're the best at what you do. And based on your conversation with Kari, he's a chauvinist, too. You gave it your best shot. It's on him that he didn't see value in working with you."

"Now what?"

"Forget it and move on."

"I guess that's all there is to do. My team's loaded with our own projects. I don't know why I even bothered with this whole thing, anyway."

"You did it because you saw a significant risk to your company that you didn't think was being addressed. You did everything you could to help them fix it. If they don't want to listen to you, that's not your problem. You did your part."

He reached across the table and took her hand. "I'm proud of you. You're the real deal."

Emily squeezed his hand as her doubts receded.

A faint rumbling snore emanated from under the table.

"I'd better get you home," Grant said. "I think you both need some sleep."

CHAPTER 29

Martha looked through the peephole on Emily's door as she pulled her robe on over her pajamas and tied the sash. No one bearing good news ever knocked on the door at five fifteen in the morning.

Dhruv stood on the other side, pacing and raking his hand through his hair.

"Dhruv," Martha said softly as she opened the door. "What's happened?"

"I need to talk to Emily." He continued to pace.

"Is Stephanie all right?"

"What? Of course she is. I need Emily."

"She's sleeping. It's very early."

"I need her."

"She didn't get home from Denver until after midnight," Martha said. She'd awakened when Emily and Garth had come in and had noted the time on her bedside clock before falling back to sleep. "Can't whatever it is wait?"

"No. She'll want to know. Wake her up." Dhruv stopped and stood in front of her, his dark eyes worried and his mouth set in a determined line she recognized from the weeks he'd spent at her own home, trying—and finally succeeding—to convince Emily to seek help at the Foundation for the Blind.

Martha nodded slowly and swung the door wide. "Come in. Zoe's still asleep. I'll go wake Emily."

Dhruv shook his head. "I need to take my dogs out. Tell Emily I'll meet her there when she brings Garth outside."

"I'm not sure she'll be taking him out, Dhruv. I suspect Emily will listen to whatever you have to say and then go back to bed."

"She won't. We'll both go to the office early."

"All right." Martha knew the futility of trying to change Dhruv's mind. "I'll tell her you're waiting for her out back."

Dhruv turned on his heel and walked to his apartment.

"DHRUV," Emily called softly as she and Garth exited from the back of their apartment building. She followed as Garth led her to his familiar spot. "What's going on?"

Sugar approached her politely while Rocco raced over to her and jumped on her leg, his front paws landing short of her knees.

"We need to work on the cyber-threat program."

Emily reached down to pet her canine friends. "Is that why you woke me? You want to start working on the program you proposed." She tried—and failed—to keep the irritation out of her voice. "I didn't get to sleep until almost two."

"Yes. We need to start. Right now."

"We won't be working on the program, Dhruv."

"We have to."

"They aren't interested in our help. They turned us down."

He stood close to her. "What happened? Wasn't my memo good enough?"

Emily put her hand on his elbow. "Your memo was perfect. They didn't listen to a word I said. Ross Wilcox had made up his mind before I even left San Francisco. This has nothing to do with the quality of your work—or the quality of my presentation," she added.

"Wilcox is an idiot," Dhruv said.

"I have to agree with you on that," Emily sighed heavily, "but cybersecurity is his department and he's made his decision."

"What did he say?"

"They've considered the risk and think it's not a credible threat. Even if there would be a breach, he feels they can handle it."

"He'll change his mind."

"No. He won't. He's not giving the issue a second thought."

"He will."

"Dhruv," Emily said, unable to conceal her frustration. "I appreciate your tenacity, but this issue is dead to us. Done. Over with."

"Not anymore."

"What do you mean? Has something happened?"

"There's been a breach. Exactly like we predicted."

"What?"

"Not at our company, but at our biggest competitor."

"How do you know this?"

"I get up early to read the news on my computer. It happened overnight. Their entire system is shut down. They've suspended trading of their stock when the market opens today."

"OMG. That's huge!"

"It's only a matter of time before it happens to us. We need to begin working."

Emily filled her lungs with air. "That doesn't change anything for us. This will be Ross's problem. We can't barge in and start working."

"So—we do nothing to help the company?"

"At the moment, that's right."

"Then what should we do?"

Emily bagged Garth's waste and placed it in the receptacle. "I'm going back to bed. Yesterday was a killer day, and I had planned to come in late this morning. I'm going to continue in that vein."

Dhruv stood in silence.

Emily turned back to the building. "I'm sorry, Dhruv. It's frustrating when corporate politics get in the way of sound decision-making, but that's how things go sometimes."

"I don't like it," he replied.

"I don't, either. At least we tried. We'll have to be satisfied with that." She walked to the door and disappeared inside.

"That's not good enough." Dhruv collected his dogs and retreated to his apartment.

CHAPTER 30

M artha was in the kitchen when we returned from our visit with Dhruv. I smelled coffee brewing halfway down the hall. Martha always got things going in the morning. My tail began to wag, thinking of my breakfast.

We stepped inside, and Emily removed my harness, hanging it on its peg by our door.

"Coffee?" Martha called.

"I'm heading right back to bed," Emily said. "If that's all right with you. Zoe should get up soon. She knows her morning routine."

"Of course. I woke when you got home last night. You'll be tired."

"Thanks, Mom," Emily said, trudging to our room.

I hesitated, looking from Emily to Martha and back again. I was torn between joining Emily for more sleep and attempting to convince Martha to feed me. I surprised myself by choosing Emily.

Emily kicked off her slippers and slid between the sheets, pulling the thick down duvet up to her nose.

I circled, then settled into my memory foam bed in the corner, burrowing my nose in the plush cover. Zoe would be up soon. I planned to rest my eyes until I heard her and Sabrina stirring on the other side of our door.

When I later opened my eyes, sun was streaming through the slit where the edges of the curtains met. The bedroom door stood open and I could hear Emily and Martha chatting.

I pushed myself to my feet and arched my back in a deep stretch. I couldn't remember ever being the last one out of bed. It was embarrassing, really. I yawned my biggest yawn and made my way to the living room.

"There you are," Emily said as I walked to where she sat on the sofa and rested my nose on her leg. "You were a sleepy boy, weren't you?" She rubbed my ears and jowls. "I was just telling Mom about our day yesterday."

I stood still, enjoying her ministrations.

"Would you like your breakfast?"

I wagged my tail.

Emily rose and headed for the cupboard that we referred to as the "dog cupboard."

Sabrina was curled into a ball, snoozing, on a spot where sunshine slanted through the living room window. She jumped up, instantly alert, and sprinted to the kitchen.

"You've already had yours, Sabrina," Martha said.

Sabrina stood next to me, anyway, hoping that Emily would ignore Martha.

Emily scooped kibble into my bowl and, at the last moment, tossed a small handful into Sabrina's bowl.

I wagged my tail harder. I liked that Emily was kind, and that Sabrina's hopefulness had been rewarded. She and I got down to business.

"I know you're not happy with how your presentation was received," Martha said. "I can understand that. But I also think you've got a lot to be proud of. You and Garth made your first trip on your own. Everything didn't go smoothly, but you handled the problems."

Emily smiled at her mother. "Thanks, Mom. I love that you always look on the bright side."

"Your father taught me that."

"I miss Dad."

"I do too. He'd be so impressed with the way you've taken control of your life, Em."

"I hope so. I think of him, up there in heaven." Emily rested her hands on the kitchen counter. "I like the fact that his organs were donated to five different people. He saved their lives."

"I do, too. It makes me feel like he's still with us."

"I agree. Do you ever hear from any of the people who received his organs?"

"No. I have a list of who they are, but I haven't kept track of them. Why—do you want to contact them?"

"No. I was just curious." She brought her hand to her mouth to stifle a yawn.

"You still look exhausted, Em. Why don't you take the day off? Stay home and rest."

"That's tempting, but I'd better go in. I checked my emails before I got out of bed and I have at least a dozen that need immediate attention. And," she pushed herself away from the counter, "if I know Dhruv, he's working away on the program he thinks will protect the company from the hackers you heard about on the morning news."

Martha chuckled. "I'll bet you're right. When he commits himself to something, there's no turning back."

Emily headed for her bedroom. "I'll be home on time tonight. Thanks for staying with Zoe. Will you go home this afternoon?"

"I'm going to spend the week here. There's a lecture at one of the libraries this afternoon, and a showing at a gallery that I'd like to take in on Wednesday. Since I'm going to stay with Zoe on Thursday night, I thought it didn't make much sense to go to my house. If you don't mind my being here."

"Of course we don't mind, Mom. As far as Zoe and I are concerned, you can move in." She turned back to face her. "I really appreciate your willingness to stay with Zoe."

"I love her like she was my own granddaughter. And I'm thrilled that you and Gina are checking in to the inn early to spend a day at the spa. You certainly deserve that."

"I feel guilty that I'm not throwing a bachelorette weekend for Gina. As maid of honor, I'm supposed to," Emily said.

"You told me Gina didn't want one."

"She's been stressed with work, the wedding, and looking

for a house with Craig. She said spending a weekend away would tip her over the edge."

"I can understand that. All the hoopla around weddings these days seems crazy to me."

"That's why Connor and I didn't have a big affair. And with the way things turned out, I'm glad we didn't spend all that money. What a waste."

The two women remained silent with their own thoughts.

"Well… that's water over the dam," Emily said. "To tell you the truth—I love my life. Zoe, Garth, Grant, you—I couldn't ask for more." She reached her bedroom door. "Except for a bit more patience from my best senior programmer."

Martha laughed. "I think Dhruv's perfect, just the way he is."

I looked up from my bowl of kibble. Once again, I had to agree with Martha. I finished eating and settled down by the door. Now that I'd eaten, I was ready to tackle the day.

CHAPTER 31

*R*honda was passing by the elevator bank when Emily and Garth stepped off.

"Hi, Em. I'm glad you're here," she said.

"Why? Is there a problem?"

"No. It's just that Dhruv has been looking for you. He's been in and out of my office every half hour since I came in this morning—asking if I'd heard from you."

"Oh, boy. He's got a burr under his saddle, doesn't he?"

"I'm afraid he does. He's bent everyone's ear about the cyberattack on our competitor—and that we need to create a program to protect our company."

"I'll go see him; try to calm him down. As you know, I went to Denver yesterday to meet with the team responsible for security threats."

"He told us what you said about the meeting. They're not interested in our help."

Emily sighed heavily.

Rhonda stepped closer. "Can you really blame them? How receptive would we be if a manager from another division flew in to tell us we didn't know what we were doing?"

"That's not how I presented it."

"I'm sure you didn't, but it sounds like that's the way their director took it."

"I guess you're right." Emily's purse slipped onto her elbow, and she hoisted it back onto her shoulder. "There's nothing more for us to do. I'll put my stuff in my office and go find Dhruv—try to redirect his attention back to our work."

"Good luck," Rhonda said. "Don't be too hard on him. His heart is in the right place."

"Always," Emily said, continuing on to her office. She'd just stowed her purse in her desk drawer and logged on to her computer when Garth's tail began beating steadily against the floor.

"Hey, Dhruv. I understand you've been looking for me."

"I've been working on the program."

"It's not our responsibility, Dhruv. I told you—they turned us down."

"There's been another breach."

"Where?"

"Not us—another competitor. It came across the news feed on my phone."

"How bad?"

"Bad. Their entire database is breached and the hackers are demanding a ransom."

"Are they going to pay?"

"I don't know. It's breaking news."

"Hackers from overseas?"

"They think so."

"Well… that's terrible. I hope it doesn't happen to us."

"What is it they say about 'hope?' That it's not a strategy."

"Dhruv!" Emily's tone was shriller than she'd intended. "We work for a multi-billion-dollar corporation. You and I don't run this place. We're minor cogs in the giant wheel. We offered our help and the security division turned it down. I'm sorry I didn't convince them. End of story."

"It's not your fault, Em. I saw your slides and our memo. They should have been convinced."

She remained silent.

"We just return to our assigned tasks and ignore the threat? That's stupid."

"I agree with you, but there it is. Stop watching the news feed—you're driving yourself nuts." She refrained from adding that he was driving everyone else on the team nuts, too. "Nothing's happened to us. Take comfort in that."

"Okay," he mumbled, eyes down. He turned to go when Emily stopped him.

"Do you remember that Zoe, Martha, Garth, and I will all be at my friend Gina's wedding this weekend?"

"Yep. You'll be gone from work on Thursday and Friday. Martha and Zoe will join you on Friday. You'll all come home on Sunday and I'm watching Sabrina for you."

"You remembered it all!"

"Of course. I don't forget things."

"Thank you. And try not to worry about a cyberattack on the company. I feel confident they're ready for anything that might happen," she said, turning her face to her computer so he couldn't see the doubt in her eyes.

CHAPTER 32

The rideshare driver pulled to a stop under the protection of the inn's porte cochere. The rain that had been pelting the car only seconds earlier suddenly ceased. The windshield wipers, turned to their highest speed, scraped against the glass.

The driver turned to Gina and Emily in the back seat. "Why don't the three of you go inside? I'll get your bags and bring them to you."

"Thank you," Gina said to the driver. "That's very thoughtful."

"The wind's blowing sideways. You'll get soaked if you don't run for it."

Emily placed Garth into his harness with practiced hands, and they dashed inside. The three waited inside the door. Garth gave himself a mighty shake, showering them with droplets of water.

The driver brought in two enormous suitcases and an oversize garment carrier.

"I'm getting married," Gina said.

The driver grinned. "I figured as much. I'll get the rest."

"I hope this clears up. We've got an outdoor wedding and reception." Gina's voice held more than a note of panic.

"You've been watching the weather maps all week," Emily said. "This storm is supposed to move on by this evening. Saturday is forecast to be beautiful."

"I know, I know. I'm just nervous."

The driver came in with another two large suitcases, a carry-on, a makeup case, and a duffel containing Garth's necessities.

"That's all of it," he said.

"Thank you so very much," Gina said, holding out a small wad of folded bills.

"Thank you! And congratulations," he said as he went out the door.

"He was nice," Emily said. "We're off to a good start."

"I hope you're right. I just don't want anything bad to happen..." Gina stopped abruptly. "Oh, Em. I can't believe I just said that. I'm worried about the weather at my wedding when you—"

"Had a riding accident that caused my retinas to detach." Emily finished her sentence for her. "It's okay, Gina. The tragedy that caused my blindness doesn't mean you shouldn't want the plans you've made for your wedding to go smoothly."

"It was insensitive of me. I'm so sorry."

Emily reached for her friend and drew her into a hug. "We'll have none of this. We're here for a relaxing spa day." She tapped her smartwatch and listened to the time. "I believe we have herbal linen wrap treatments in thirty minutes."

Gina squeezed her hard before releasing her. "We do. Let's check in and head to the spa."

"Will our rooms be ready this early?"

"I don't think so," Gina said. "The porters will hold our luggage and take it to our rooms."

"Right."

"I just hope they don't lose my wedding dress!"

"No negative thoughts," Emily admonished. "Everything is going to be perfect."

CHAPTER 33

I hoped we would come back here. My Emily was more relaxed than she'd been in months. I, myself, don't have a problem relaxing, but even I'd felt the calming effects of this place.

I remembered that Emily called it a spa. Frosted-glass wall sconces and dozens of candles scattered on every flat surface provided diffuse lighting. Slow-paced music played faintly in the background. Based upon my one visit to the symphony, I thought it was strings. The temperature was pleasantly cool—probably to accommodate the thick terry cloth robes worn by the patrons.

I'd tried to stay awake during the herbal linen wrap treatment Gina and Emily had started their spa day with—and then again during the facials that followed. There was something about this place that forced my eyelids shut. I was powerless to resist.

I awoke with a start when Emily swung her legs off the edge of the table at the conclusion of her facial.

"He's had a good nap, hasn't he?" The facialist handed Emily a piece of paper. "Here's the list of the products I recommend. You've got lovely skin. You don't need much."

Emily stood and grasped my handle. "Thank you. I'll be sure to buy one of each when we're done."

"Your schedule says that you and your friend are meeting at our in-spa café for lunch. I'll take you there."

"Thank you. I haven't done anything except lie around all morning, but I'm famished."

"Everyone says that. Follow me."

We soon entered a round atrium in the middle of the spa. Rain plunked against a large skylight. Small tables swathed in crisp white linen cloths ringed a central fountain. We were shown to our table, and a server placed water glasses in front of Gina and Emily.

I gazed longingly at the water. Round slices of what looked like orange, lemon, lime, and cucumber floated in each glass.

"Would you mind bringing water to my service dog?" Emily asked, as if reading my mind.

"Of course. I'll have to get tap water from the kitchen. The only water we have in here is spa water."

I brought my nose up to look at the server, trying to telegraph my thoughts to her. I'd be open to trying some of that spa water.

She turned and hurried to the kitchen, returning with a

bowl of water. Spa—or not—it tasted great. I quenched my thirst and settled under the table.

"I want to hear all about your house hunting," Emily said after they'd placed their orders for grilled salmon Cobb salads.

"We're under contract to buy a four-bedroom, two-and-a-half-bath single-family home close to Craig's veterinary practice."

"You didn't tell me! That's exciting."

"Everything's been so busy. We started the process months ago and kept getting outbid. I never thought we'd end up with this one. We'd even decided to suspend our search until after the wedding if this didn't work out."

"But you had the winning bid?"

"Yep. I'm thrilled—it's my favorite of all the houses we looked at. We'll have plenty of room for a family in this one."

"You see? Things work out as they're supposed to. When do you move in?"

"We close escrow when we're on our honeymoon and I have to be out of my apartment two weeks after we get back."

"Wow! You are busy. Zoe and I can help you pack."

"Thank you. I may take you up on that."

"Tell me all about the house. I want every detail."

Gina launched into a description of flooring and flow, crown molding and cabinets. My eyelids became impossibly heavy, and I succumbed to sleep.

Emily once again woke me by grasping my harness. "It

sounds like the rain has stopped. I'm going to ask where I can take Garth for a comfort break."

"Good idea," Gina said. "We've got an hour before our massages. I'll check to see if our rooms are ready."

Both women entered the locker room and exchanged their fluffy robes for the clothes they'd worn that morning.

Emily and I walked down a long corridor with doorways on either side until we came to a set of glass double doors at the end. The porter led us to a grassy area to our right.

"Would you like me to stay to see you back to the spa?" he asked.

"No thanks. We can find it."

I stretched my legs on the spongy grass. Unlike my finicky friend Sabrina, I like the feel of water on my paws and mud between my toes. I was headed toward a brown patch in a low spot of the lawn when Emily commanded me to do my business. I put my mind back on the task at hand and did as I was told. A frolic in the mud wasn't what we were here for.

I finished, and Emily bagged my waste. I took her to a trash can by the sidewalk and she threw it away.

"Can you find the spa?" Emily asked.

Was she kidding me? Of course I could. I'd memorized "spa" and hoped we'd return.

We got back to the spa before Gina. Emily had me take her to the locker room, and she quickly traded her clothes for the robe. Gina joined us as Emily was securing the lock on her locker. I could tell the minute I spotted Gina that something was very wrong.

"You're back. Were our rooms ready?"

"Yes." Gina's voice wavered.

"What's wrong? Aren't they the right ones?"

"They're what I reserved. And they're very nice."

"You're upset. I can tell."

"It's just that our luggage was in our rooms—all of it, except my dress!" She ended on a sob.

I got to my feet and hovered near Emily. We'd jump in to fix whatever was upsetting our friend Gina. I was certain of it.

"You're sure? You checked everywhere?"

"Of course I did," Gina snapped. "Sorry, Em. I didn't mean to sound so snippy. I'm just freaked out."

"I understand." Emily stood and grasped my harness. "Come on. We're going up there to look again." Emily commanded me to move forward.

"You're in your robe," Gina observed.

"I don't care. A missing wedding dress is an emergency. Let's go."

Gina led the way. Emily and I walked our fastest. I knew we were on a mission.

We entered a large room with an enormous bed in the middle. French doors led to a veranda overlooking the ocean. A mound of luggage stood against one wall. Mirrored accordion doors stood open, displaying an empty closet.

"Still not here?"

"No. The closet is over here and it's empty." Gina's voice was shrill.

"Are there other closets?"

"No."

"Let's check my room."

"They put our luggage in the correct rooms. I don't think..." Gina began.

"We're going to check. If it's not in my room, then we're going to turn this inn upside down until we find your dress. Don't worry."

I opened my mouth and began to pant, even though I wasn't warm and hadn't exerted myself. I sensed we were dealing with a big issue, but I couldn't make out what it was.

Gina led us to a door along the corridor next to hers. "You're in the upgraded suite that they set aside for the bride."

"What in the world?" Emily asked. "Why didn't you keep the upgrade for yourself?"

"I don't need it, but you do. You've got Martha and Zoe with you tomorrow and Saturday nights, plus Garth. You're the one who can use the extra space."

"That's very generous of you." Emily stood in the center of the room.

"You're in a small sitting room," Gina said. "The two bedrooms with attached baths open off this room on either side."

"Is there a closet in here?"

"No."

"I had your luggage put in the room to your right. I checked the closet. My dress isn't there."

"Go check the other closet," Emily said.

Gina was already on her way. "It makes no sense that they

would have hung it in—" her words stopped suddenly, followed by a whoop of pleasure. "It's here!"

"Thank goodness," Emily called to her.

I could feel the tension ease out of Emily as she relaxed her grip on my harness. She'd been calm on the outside, but she couldn't fool me. She'd been worried about whatever had upset Gina.

"Oh, Em," Gina said. "Thanks for insisting we come right up. I was freaking out." She walked out of the room, holding the garment bag with her dress high over her head. "Why in the world did they put it in that closet?"

"This is the suite they reserved for the bride, silly. They didn't know you'd be so kind and generous and give it to your best friend."

Gina blew out a big breath. "Whew. What would I have done without my dress?"

"We'd have come up with something. You're getting married Saturday, no matter what."

"Thanks for being such a good sport and traipsing through the inn in a robe."

Emily laughed. "To tell you the truth, I *was* a bit worried. Now—I think if we hurry, we can make it back to the spa in time for our massages."

"I'm in favor of that. Let me put my dress in my room and we'll be on our way."

Gina hurried to her room as I looked up at Emily. I was glad that we were headed back to the spa—we all needed it.

CHAPTER 34

"Look at this room!" Zoe twirled in the center of the sitting room. "And it's got bedrooms, too. I didn't know there were hotel rooms like this."

"It's called a suite," Emily said. "The Inn provided it to the bride, but she gave it to us."

"This is spectacular," Martha said, walking to the wall of blackout curtains and pulling them aside. Sun flooded the room. She opened the door to the large balcony that, like the one off of Gina's room next door, had a view of the ocean. "Gina told me she was going to give us the suite."

"Why didn't you tell me?" Emily asked.

"Gina wanted it to be a surprise."

"It certainly was." Emily sank onto the love seat in the sitting room.

Martha settled next to her. "What did you do today?"

"Not much. I didn't wake up until after ten. The bed is

wonderful. I'm going to find out where I can buy the duvet they use. I slept like a log last night. Gina and I had lunch and then I came back here."

"You weren't working away on your laptop?"

Emily reached out and folded the screen closed on the laptop perched on the coffee table in front of her.

"I thought you planned to unplug completely for a few days," Martha said.

"I did—I do. Starting now." She slid the laptop toward her mother. "You can take it away from me, if you want to."

Martha laughed. "What do you think?" she called to Zoe, who was exploring the suite.

"Yes! Do it. She'll be checking on work if we don't," came the echoing reply from one of the cavernous bathrooms.

"This is going to be such a fun weekend for us all," Martha said.

Zoe joined them, walking onto the balcony. "This is so cool."

"There are two beds in our room," Martha said to Zoe. "You can take your pick."

"I want the one by the window," Zoe said.

"It's yours," Martha said. "You'd better get changed. The two of you need to head to the rehearsal in half an hour."

"Aren't you coming?" Emily asked.

"I'm going to put my feet up on the chaise lounge on this balcony and watch the ocean until it's time for the rehearsal dinner."

"That sounds like a good plan." Emily pushed herself to her feet. "I'll go make myself presentable."

"You mean make yourself beautiful for Grant?" Zoe teased.

"Come on, Zoe," Martha interjected. "Let's get your slacks and blouse out for tonight."

Thirty minutes later, Emily, Zoe, and Garth emerged from their room. They were almost at the elevator when a familiar male voice called to them.

"Grant," Emily turned in his direction.

"Hi, Diedre," Zoe said.

"Are you on our floor?" Diedre asked.

"Next to Gina," Zoe said.

"We're right across from her," Diedre said.

"We've got a great big room with lots of other rooms. It's called a suite," Zoe said.

"That sounds neat. We've got a regular room."

"Wanna see it when we're done?"

"Sure." The two girls put their heads together and chattered.

Grant leaned in to Emily and kissed her lightly on the top of the head. "Looks like these two are getting along," he said softly.

"Gina worked her magic," Emily replied.

The elevator pinged and the doors opened. They all got on.

"Who knows? Maybe this weekend will cement a lot of relationships." Grant pushed the button for the lobby and the elevator began to move.

~

"DINNER WAS MARVELOUS." Martha stood next to Sylvia at the elevator bank. "That mushroom risotto was the best I've had. Thank you for including me."

"Of course," Sylvia replied. "The food here is top-notch. Wait until you taste the Cornish game hens we're having for dinner at the reception." She glanced over her shoulder to where Emily and Grant huddled together at the edge of the group, waiting to take the elevator to their floor. "Who knows—we might become extended family, one of these days."

Martha followed Sylvia's gaze, over the heads of the wedding party, to where her daughter stood. "They certainly seem happy together, don't they?"

"Absolutely. I'm doubly thrilled this weekend. Craig is marrying Gina, whom I already love like the daughter we never had, and Grant will have more time with Emily." She cleared her throat and her voice was husky. "I only wish my husband had lived to see this day."

Martha put her arm around the woman's shoulders and gave her a half hug. "I'm a widow, myself. I can imagine how you're feeling."

The elevator chimed, and the doors opened. Sylvia and Martha stepped into the elevator, together with Gina's parents and Gina and Craig. Zoe and Diedre squeezed themselves in.

"You two will need to catch the next one," Craig called to his brother, who didn't give any indication he'd heard or cared. "I don't think they even know we're here," Craig said as the elevator doors closed.

The elevator climbed to their floor, and everyone disembarked, murmuring the usual pleasantries about the big day tomorrow.

"Can I show Diedre our suite?" Zoe asked.

Martha looked at the two sets of pleading eyes trained on her. She knew she should say no—it was late, and they all needed to go to bed. She turned to Sylvia. "What do you think?"

Sylvia sided with the girls. "Why not? The rehearsal and dinner were so much fun. I suspect it's going to be a while before anyone calms down enough to go to sleep."

Martha unlocked their door, and the girls rushed in. Zoe started the tour in the sitting room, excitedly supplying details about the rooms that would have done justice to a real estate agent showing the property to a prospective buyer.

"Would you like to come in—and talk?" Martha asked Sylvia.

"I'd enjoy getting to know you better, but I'm already two hours past my bedtime. I need to turn in."

Martha chuckled. "I'm an early riser, too. Even though I'm staying up late, I'll wake up before six and won't be able to go back to sleep."

"Another thing we have in common."

Martha swung to Sylvia. "What are you doing for breakfast?"

"I thought I'd order room service. I don't want to eat in the dining room by myself. Not on Craig's wedding day."

"Why don't we meet downstairs for breakfast? I'm sure

I'll wake up hours earlier than Emily and Zoe. I'm planning to go downstairs because I won't want to wake them with room service bringing in their clattering cart." Martha smiled at Sylvia. "You'd be doing me a favor. I won't have to eat alone."

"I'd love that," Sylvia replied, returning Martha's smile. "Seven? I'm getting my hair done at nine."

"Perfect. We'll be finished in plenty of time."

"Thank you, Martha. This will make tomorrow less lonely for me."

The two women looked at each other as the familiar bonds of friendship enfolded them.

"We've got an idea!" Zoe said as the two girls rejoined Martha and Sylvia in the hallway. "We both think it's great."

Diedre hovered close to Zoe, their shoulders touching.

The girls related their plan to the two women, interrupting each other and interjecting reasons why theirs was a good idea.

Sylvia raised an eyebrow and slanted her gaze to Martha.

"I think that's a wonderful idea!" Martha said. "But you'll have to ask Emily and your dad."

"Ask us what?" Emily inquired as she, Grant, and Garth approached.

"I didn't see you there," Martha said.

"It looked like these two were making quite a sales pitch," Grant said. "No wonder you didn't hear us approaching. What's up?"

Zoe and Diedre joined hands. "We want Diedre to stay in our room. With us," Zoe said.

"It could be a real girl's night," Diedre added.

"I don't know, honey," Emily replied. "Martha might not want…"

"I've already said yes," Martha interjected. "I don't mind."

"It'll be like the ones you and Gina used to have."

Emily couldn't suppress the smile generated by all the fond memories of her happy childhood with Gina.

"Rooming with two noisy little girls, whispering to each other? You'll never get to sleep. Why don't you move into my room with me, Mom? There's plenty of room in the king-size bed for both of us."

"We'd have our very own room—all to ourselves!" Zoe gushed.

"You'd have to promise me you'll get ready for bed right away. Lights out—and no more talking—in an hour. You've both got a big day tomorrow." Emily's tone was stern.

"We promise!" both girls said in unison.

"Moving to your room works for me," Martha said.

"Daaaad? Can I?"

All female eyes were on him.

"I can't possibly say no to all of you. I'll bring your stuff over."

The girls threw their arms around each other, then tore off to their room.

"With that, I'm headed to bed. See you at breakfast, Martha." Sylvia walked down the hall to her room.

"I'm going to move my makeup and clothes to your room, Em." Martha left Grant and Emily in the hall.

"I'm sorry that you're now going to be left all alone,"

Emily said.

Grant pulled her to him. "I could help with the conges-tion in your suite," he said, trailing kisses by her ear. "You could move over here with me."

Emily leaned into him, enjoying the tingling sensations aroused by his lips. "Under these circumstances? I don't think so."

He stepped back. "I had to try."

"And I'm glad you did." Emily cuffed him playfully on the arm. "Let's get Diedre's things. I need to get them settled."

Grant emerged from their room with Diedre's suitcase, backpack, and garment bag. "You gals don't travel light, even when you're only ten, do you?"

"Not when we're in a wedding, no."

He took the things into the suite and followed the high-pitched voices to Zoe's room. Grant met up with Emily in the sitting room. "Good luck getting those two asleep in an hour."

"Honestly, I'm not too worried about it. I'm a night owl, so I'd be up, anyway." She lowered her voice. "I'm thrilled that they're getting along so well. Zoe hasn't had any close girlfriends."

"I'm pleased, too. Zoe's a very nice girl. She's smart, caring, and focused. That's the kind of friend I'd like Diedre to have."

Grant placed two fingers under Emily's chin and lifted her face for a gentle kiss. "See you tomorrow at the wedding. And if you change your mind and decide you're too crowded over here, I'm right across the hall."

CHAPTER 35

a s far as I could see, these women were all losing their minds. After staying up way too late, this morning Emily had gotten up right after Martha left—and the first thing she did was give me a bath! I almost never need a bath and certainly didn't need one then. My coat stays naturally clean.

I had no sooner finished my breakfast when Emily led me into the large, jetted tub. She lathered me up and sprayed me down with a shower nozzle that detached from the wall. She'd taken a bath our first night here and used the jets in this tub. I remembered the rumbling sound it made, and all the mountains of bubbles it had produced. I'd been hoping for the same treatment, but apparently we didn't have time.

Martha came back from breakfast, and Emily tasked her with brushing my coat. I heard Emily tell Martha that she, Zoe, and Diedre had to be at the spa by nine. They were all getting manicures, pedicures, and their hair styled. Emily was also getting her makeup done. It soon became apparent that I wasn't going. I'd been perfectly behaved when I'd been at the spa the day before, so was at a loss as to why I was being excluded.

Martha told Emily to text her when the girls were finished and that she'd bring them back to the room so they didn't have to wait at the spa for Emily to be done.

Everything eventually went as planned. After a delightfully long session with Martha and my brush, I curled up on the carpet in front of the open balcony door, the warm breeze drying my coat thoroughly.

I cracked open an eye when the room service trolley arrived in the early afternoon. All my girls were swathed in thick white robes furnished by the inn. Although the trolley was loaded with food, none of them sat down to eat. The girls grazed and Martha filled a plate, but Emily ignored the food, replying to Martha's admonition that she ought to eat something with a vague promise that she'd eat in a second. That second never came.

Martha looked normal to me, but that's as far as it went. The girls had each had their hair curled and pinned behind their ears with beaded hair pins. Emily's thick auburn mane had been swept back from her face and folded in an intricate braid that was secured to the crown of her head with the same beaded hair pins.

Emily's beautiful eyes had been outlined in a dark shade of brown and her eyelashes were a heavy black. She looked glamorous—like the celebrities whose photos were plastered on the side of the buses we rode when we went out—but I preferred her without all the extra makeup. The loving, kind expression in those eyes was all anyone needed.

I stared at Emily as she sat on the edge of a chair, her arms circling herself. A palpable sadness lodged itself behind her expression. She ignored the chaos around us. Unlike dogs, who live in the present, I knew people had unhappy memories that made them sad. I was pretty sure Emily was going somewhere bad in her mind—to a time when I hadn't been in her life.

The sun had grown hot, and I was uncomfortably warm. I moved closer to the room service trolley, hoping someone would break the rules and feed me table scraps. I soon realized that wasn't going to happen, so I relocated to the corner on the far side of the sitting room.

I'd scored people-food at the rehearsal dinner and should be content with that. A hand had appeared under the table, holding an entire filet mignon steak under my nose. Based on the familiar ring on her left hand, I recognized it as Gina's. I'm not allowed to have table food and I should have refused. But snitching on the bride-to-be seemed to me to be very bad form, so I accepted her offering and kept her secret. It was the decent thing to do.

It seemed like I'd just closed my eyes when Emily was waking me up and putting my harness around my neck. I looked at her. The robe was gone, and she was resplendent in a long, sleek column of shimmery, rich teal. She was, without question, the most beautiful woman in the world.

"Do you have his bow tie, Zoe?" Emily turned her head over her shoulder.

"Right here." Zoe handed Emily a thin, flat bow in fabric that matched Emily's dress. "Do you need help?"

Emily was running her hands along my collar until she came to the ring that held my tags. She separated two sets of Velcro tabs and secured the bow to my collar, turning it so the bow was under my chin.

"There," she said, standing and turning to face the room. "How do we look?"

"Fabulous," Martha said, smiling broadly while dabbing at her eyes with a tissue.

"Are you girls both ready?"

"We are," they replied.

"You all look beautiful," Martha said. "Diedre—that dress is lovely on you. And Zoe, the pantsuit is elegant and suits you to a T. Good choices, girls."

"Thanks, Mom," Emily said. She addressed the girls. "Remember what we talked about last night? Being junior bridesmaids is a big responsibility. Your job doesn't end after you've walked down the aisle."

"We know," Zoe said. "We've been talking about it. Since Gina didn't hire a wedding planner, we can be extra helpers."

"Like telling guests where to put wedding presents, and knowing where the restrooms are," Diedre added. "Zoe put it on her phone and sent it to me."

"I'm glad you're taking this so seriously." Emily smiled at the enthusiasm for their tasks. "You'll be a big help—I know it. Remember to have fun, too."

"We will. We're going to dance together, like you said."

"Good! So many men don't like to dance that women dance together all the time."

"I think it's time we all headed out," Martha said. "The wedding party needs to be there on time."

We moved to the door and down the corridor. I was gratified to see all the admiring glances from other guests and staff at the inn. We all looked fabulous—especially Emily.

CHAPTER 36

A fireball of a sun was sinking toward the horizon over the Pacific Ocean, painting ribbons of purple and crimson on the high clouds. Rows of white wooden chairs were arranged in rows facing a wedding arch adorned with white and cream roses and swathed in tulle. Bows decorated with roses and trailing ivy were tied to the chairs along the aisle. A warm breeze blew in from the ocean.

One hundred twenty-five people, resplendent in tailored suits and frothy dresses, sat in the chairs. Sylvia and Hilary had both been seated. The air of happy expectancy was palpable.

Zoe stood at the back of the aisle that separated the seats into the traditional bride's and groom's sections. The satin of her jumpsuit shone in the light of the setting sun. Diedre was behind her, elegant in her lace dress with the twirly skirt.

Both girls held simple nosegays of white roses and lily of the valley, tied with shimmery teal ribbons.

Emily held Garth's harness with her left hand and had taken Grant's arm with her right. A matching corsage was secured to her wrist and Garth's bow tie sported the same boutonniere that Grant wore in his lapel.

The strains of Pachelbel's "Canon in D" soared over the assembly.

The pastor stepped from the right side to the center of the arch. Craig followed him.

Zoe kept her eyes trained on Craig until he reached his spot.

He turned to her and nodded slightly.

Zoe recognized her cue. She stared at the chairs, now full of people whose faces were turned to her. Her hands began to tremble, and the bouquet slipped from her grasp. She caught it before it hit the ground. Zoe inhaled deeply and began her trip down the aisle.

Diedre came next. Both girls turned to the left before they reached the arch and took their assigned places.

Grant squeezed Emily's hand. She commanded Garth to move forward, and they began walking to the majestic music. Grant kept his hand on hers until he'd seen her to her spot next to where Gina would stand. Then he joined his brother.

The music transitioned to the traditional wedding march. The pastor invited everyone to rise. Gina, in a delicate lace dress with a sweetheart neckline, fitted bodice, and graceful train, made her way down the aisle on the arm of her father,

Charles. She kissed him before he shook Craig's hand and retreated to the pew to join Hilary.

Gina walked to Emily and pressed her bouquet into Emily's hands. The two girls stood, hands locked, for an instant.

"I'm so glad you're here, Em," Gina whispered.

"Always. Be happy," Emily whispered back.

Diedre brushed a tear off her cheek.

Gina joined her groom.

Craig leaned toward her. "You're stunning," he whispered so only she could hear.

"Dearly beloved," the pastor intoned the familiar words, and the ceremony began.

"You may kiss the bride," the pastor said.

Craig lifted the shoulder-length front portion of Gina's veil off her face and the two who had just become one sealed their union with a long, lingering kiss.

The sun dipped below the horizon and Mendelssohn's "Wedding March" rang out. Gina took her bouquet from Emily before linking arms with Craig. The beaming newly-weds walked back down the aisle together, smiling at their guests.

Fairy lights circling the trees, framing the setting, sprang into illumination as Emily followed, with Garth and Grant on either side of her.

Diedre and Zoe walked behind at a dignified pace.

Hilary and Charles were next. Sylvia rose from her seat, dabbing at her eyes with an old-fashioned lace hankie. She caught Martha's eye as she passed by.

Martha gave her an encouraging smile.

The wedding party arranged themselves in a receiving line at the entrance to the walled garden set for the reception. Round tables draped in teal linens ringed a dance floor in the center of the space. A long rectangular table dressed in white lace stood on a raised platform opposite a bar staffed with two tuxedoed bartenders. Clusters of votive candles on every table complimented the welcoming glow created by the fairy lights and party lights on long strings that crisscrossed overhead.

Wedding guests filed through the receiving line and into the garden to find their seat assignment and accept a drink or hors d'oeuvre from servers circulating with trays.

The photographer collected the wedding party and the parents of the bride and groom for photos as soon as the last guest in line had moved away. "It's the blue hour—the light is perfect. We took most of our formal photos earlier, but I'll want you for another half hour."

The photographer and his assistant worked with rhythmic precision, posing, grouping, and snapping pictures. "Thanks, everybody," the photographer said. "That's a wrap. You're all naturals in front of the camera. Now—go join the reception and we'll keep taking pictures there."

"This is when we tell the DJ they're coming." Zoe turned to Diedre, who nodded. The two girls took off at a run.

Charles offered one arm to his wife and the other to Sylvia and escorted them both into the reception.

"Go ahead," Emily said to Gina. "Everyone's waiting for you both. I'm going to give Garth a break."

"We'll be along shortly," Grant said, clapping his twin brother on the back and drawing him into a hug. "Well done, bro."

"Everything's been perfect." Emily turned toward Gina.

"It's all gone as planned," Gina said. "No glitches. I'm so relieved."

Gina and Craig walked to the garden and stood in the glow of the tall sconces that marked the entrance.

The DJ interrupted the soft classical music playing in the background. "Ladies and gentlemen, please welcome our newlyweds, Mr. and Mrs..."

A loud bang sounded from the far side of the inn. The sound system shut down, and the lights went out. The garden was plunged into darkness, broken only by the meager light from the votive candles.

Applause for the newlyweds was replaced by scattered conversations, wondering what had happened.

Grant, Emily, and Garth had just stepped onto the pathway that led to the garden.

Grant stopped walking.

"What's wrong?" Emily asked.

"The lights have gone out. It's pitch black here. I need to let my eyes adjust."

Emily chuckled. "Not a problem for Garth and me. We can lead you."

"That's true."

"Is it just the lights along this walkway, or has the power gone out on the entire property?"

Grant turned in a circle. "As far as I can tell, it's affecting the entire property."

"That's not good."

"I'm sure they'll get it up and running in no time. They'll have backup generators."

"I hope so."

"Let's get to Craig and Gina so we can find out what's going on," Grant said.

"Garth will have no problem guiding us, will you, boy? We worked on learning where the garden was when we came to the rehearsal yesterday." Emily commanded Garth to find the garden and they set off.

CHAPTER 37

"Gosh—it's so dark!" Diedre said to Zoe. "Do you think it's supposed to be?"

"No. This is wrong."

"I can kinda see Gina and Craig at the entrance," Diedre said.

"Are they kissing—again?" Zoe giggled.

"No. They've turned to each other. It looks like they're talking."

Zoe looked at the couple. "Gina's waving her arms around like she does when she's upset."

"Look at the people at the tables," Diedre said. "They're all talking, too. I hope my grandma is okay. She doesn't see well in the dark."

"My grandma was like that, too. She didn't drive at night."

"Those teeny candles don't give much light."

"Their cell phone flashlights will." Zoe turned to Diedre.

"Let's go around the tables and get everyone to turn on their flashlights and place the phones on the tables, facing up."

"That's a great idea. I'm not sure my grandma even knows how to turn her flashlight on."

"Then we'll show her how."

"Do you think it's okay if we do this? Should we ask first?"

"Emily told us junior bridesmaids are supposed to help make things run smoothly. This is exactly what we should do." Zoe squared her shoulders. "Come on. I'll go to the right, and you take the left. We'll have this place lit up in no time."

The girls moved quickly from table to table, supplying direction and receiving congratulations on their ingenious solution, until the garden glowed in a fashion more reminiscent of a rock concert than a wedding reception.

Emily and Grant caught up to Gina and Craig, who were by that time in deep conversation with the manager of the inn.

"What do you mean, the backup generators only power the lights and heating and cooling for the main building?" Gina's voice was shrill. "What about out here?"

"We're bringing every candle we can lay our hands on," the man said.

"You said that the power outage is affecting more than the inn," Craig said. "Do you have any idea when the utility will restore power?"

"We've called and all we get is a recording that says they're aware of the outage and crews are working on restoring power."

"So, we have no idea?" Craig sounded as anxious as Gina.

"No, sir. I'm sorry."

Grant spoke up. "Look what the girls have done." He pointed into the garden. "At least there's enough light for the guests to move around and the servers to finish passing the hors d'oeuvres."

"I hadn't noticed," Gina said. "That was resourceful of them. Once you bring out more candles, we'll have enough light for dinner."

The manager cleared his throat. "That's the other thing."

Gina, Craig, Emily, and Grant all swung to face him.

"Our ovens are electric. We'd just started the entrées, but we won't be able to finish them if the power doesn't come back on in the next few minutes."

Gina put her hands on the manager's lapels, pushing her bouquet into his chest. "You're telling me I have one hundred twenty-five wedding guests who are expecting a meal in the next thirty minutes, and you CAN'T SERVE THEM?"

"Come on, honey. It's not his fault." Craig put his arm around her shoulder.

She shrugged it off. "What's your Plan B?" She elevated her five-foot-three-inch frame onto her tiptoes and leaned menacingly toward the manger.

"We can still serve the salads. We'll finish plating them by candlelight. It may take us a bit longer, but we can do it. And," the four gathered around him heard him gulp, "we'll order in... pizza."

"WHAT?" Gina shrieked, a drop of spittle flying from her mouth and landing on the manager's chin.

The man took a step back.

"That's a great idea," Grant said. "Not pizza, of course," he added quickly. "What about food trucks?"

Gina lowered her heels to the ground.

"That's a very 'in' thing to do these days," Emily agreed. "It could be fun."

"Do you have any food trucks you can call in?" Craig asked the manager.

The man stuck a finger inside his collar and loosed the button under his tie. "I'm afraid not."

Gina moaned. "I don't want pizza!"

"Then dinner consists of salad and wedding cake. We always order salads when we go out to dinner," Emily reminded her, "and we usually split a dessert. This will be the same thing."

"I think I can come up with food trucks," Grant said. "My architectural firm deals with several food truck companies that service our building sites." He pulled out his cell phone and began scrolling. "I've got a list of companies right here. We steer them a lot of business. Let me make some calls and see if we can get a couple of trucks here."

"Okay," Gina said. "That would work. Dinner delayed is better than dinner cancelled, but what will everyone do in the meantime?"

Craig snapped his fingers. "Dance! We'll get this party started."

"We don't have power for the DJ," Gina almost hissed.

"Yeah, we do. You know that electric truck I just bought? It's in the parking lot. The battery can power a house for up to three days. I'm sure it can handle the DJ—and the lights in the garden, too." Craig turned to his brother. "Grant and I will take it from here."

"Well done, you two," Emily said. She turned to Gina. "Why don't we sneak back to your room? You can touch up your makeup and have some water. By the time we get back here, everything will be fixed."

"That's a wonderful idea," the manager chimed in.

Grant and Craig had already moved off to accomplish their tasks.

"Will you make sure the guests know what's happening?" Emily addressed the manager.

"Of course."

Emily took Gina's elbow. "Find our room, Garth."

The manager, clearly relieved, headed in one direction while Garth led his girls in the other.

I WAS MAKING good time toward the main building of the inn when Gina stopped abruptly. "Let's not."

"Not what?" Emily asked.

"Go to your room. It's on the second floor and the elevator won't be working because of the power outage. I'm not going up and down stairs in my wedding gown."

"Fair enough. Do you want to go right back to the reception?"

"Not yet. My car's in the lot and I keep a stash of makeup

and a brush in my glove box. We can sit there for a few minutes while I fix my face."

"Good idea." Emily commanded me to follow Gina and the two of them were soon seated in the front of Gina's car while I sprawled out along the length of the back seat. The leather upholstery felt smooth and cool against my fur. I felt myself grow weary and fought against it. I wanted to stay alert for my girls.

Gina unzipped the pouch with her makeup and turned on the overhead light inside the car. She picked up a round container of blush, then replaced it without opening it. "This is a dumb idea. I'll get makeup powder all over my dress."

"I'm sure you look fine, Gina. You don't need more makeup. People won't see it in the dark, anyway."

Gina swiped across her lips with a tube of lip gloss before returning it to the pouch and replacing the pouch in the glove box. "Tonight gave me a tiny glimpse into what your world must be like, Em."

Emily placed her hands in her lap and shrugged. "I guess."

"It's so strange that it happened at my wedding."

"I guess we both have strange karma with weddings and not being able to see," Emily said.

I could tell that she was trying to sound nonchalant.

"Has all this—my wedding—been hard on you, Em? Has it brought back memories?"

They sat in silence.

Emily's voice was ragged when she finally spoke. "Maybe a little. I remembered how happy and hopeful I was when I said my 'I do's' with Connor. I felt secure in the path that my life would take."

"Except by the next day, you'd had your riding accident, your retinas were detaching, and you lost your sight."

"With the end of my marriage not far behind."

"Plus, you thought that Connor and I were having an affair."

Emily reached a hand across the console and touched Gina's arm. "And I was wrong about that. The short answer to your question is that your wedding has brought back memories. Most of them aren't happy ones." She took a breath, and her voice was strong. "It's also reminded me of how far I've come—of how much I have in my life to be thankful for."

As she continued, I saw Emily square her shoulders. "I have Zoe now, and she means the world to me. My team is the best and I am killing it at work. I'm spending more time with Mom. You and I are besties again. And Garth," she reached a hand over the back seat to rub behind my ears, "is my everything."

I pressed my head into her hand. I knew we had an unbreakable bond, but it was still gratifying to hear her say so.

"Oh, Em. I'm so glad to hear you say all of this."

"Your wedding was beautiful, Gina. I'm delighted that you've married Craig. You've got yourself a fantastic guy, and I know you're going to build a very happy life together."

"Thank you. He's my soul mate." Gina sighed contentedly. "I have one more question."

"Oh?"

"You didn't mention Grant in the things you're thankful for?"

Emily laughed. "It's all so new, it's hard to believe it's real, but yes—I'm falling for Grant, and I think he's falling for me."

"Fallen, you mean. As far as I can see, the two of you have fallen for each other."

Gina had gotten that right.

Emily laughed. "Time will tell. I think the bride's had enough time to powder her nose. We'd better get back before they send out a search party for us."

"Good idea," Gina said. "I'm glad we had these few minutes alone to chat."

"Me too. Are you feeling better? No matter what's happened, we're going to have a fabulous time at your reception. Are you with me?"

"One thousand percent, and always," Gina said.

We all piled out of the car, and I took the lead. I was ready to party, too.

We were thirty feet from the entrance to the walled garden when the overhead lights sprang to life. Cheers and applause erupted from the wedding guests. The DJ announced that food trucks would be arriving shortly, and that the bar was open. More cheers and another round of applause followed.

Craig intercepted us at the entrance and took Gina's hand. "The salads have been served and the food trucks will be here in less than an hour. The DJ agrees that we start the dancing before dinner. What do you say?"

"Great idea. That'll give people something to do while they wait."

Craig planted a kiss into Gina's palm before he made the thumbs up sign at the DJ and walked to the middle of the dance floor.

The DJ nodded in acknowledgment. His microphone crackled. "While we wait for dinner, let's get this party started. Put your hands together for Mr. and Mrs. Craig Johnson!"

Craig extended his hand to Gina. She entered the dance floor. He turned her with a flourish before taking her into his arms. The beginning notes of "Make You Feel My Love" filled the air. The guests left their seats and gathered to watch the couple.

Gina and Craig circled the floor, then settled in the center, their foreheads touching. Craig cupped Gina's chin in his hands and raised it to kiss her as they swayed to the music. Applause erupted from the onlookers.

The first dance concluded as Craig dipped Gina, then spun her away to her father's waiting arms. The DJ played "Isn't She Lovely." Charles Roberts grinned at his daughter as they took off around the floor. Craig pulled Sylvia to her feet to join them. When the DJ started the next tune, guests poured onto the floor to gyrate to "Don't Stop Believin.'"

Everyone was partying when the DJ stopped the music to announce that Modern Taco and Dragon Flame were stationed in the parking lot. "You're in for a treat, folks. I'm a fan of both food trucks. They're fabulous. We'll let the bride and groom go first, followed by the wedding party and parents of the bride and groom. After that, it's first come, first served. And I'll keep playing tunes. I can see that some of you don't want to leave the dance floor."

Zoe and Diedre joined Emily and Grant in line. Emily bent and spoke to them both. The girls nodded their understanding and raced ahead to intercept Gina and Craig at Modern Taco.

"We'll carry your plates to the table for you," Diedre said.

"You don't want to spill on your clothes," Zoe added.

"That's very thoughtful of you," Gina said.

"Tell us what you want, and we'll bring it to you," Diedre said.

The newlyweds complied and headed back to the walled garden and their table.

Grant turned to Emily. "Those girls are having the time of their lives."

"I'm so glad—I was afraid they'd be bored."

"They would have been, without each other. They've taken their responsibilities as junior bridesmaids very seriously. We may have a couple of future wedding planners on our hands."

Emily chuckled. "And to think I made that all up just to keep them busy."

"Genius idea." Grant circled her with his arms as they inched forward in line.

"How about you? Are you having fun?" Emily leaned back against him. "You must be thinking about Diedre's mother."

"I've thought about her—and our wedding, of course. Those are good memories for me—but they're just that. Memories." Grant rested his chin on the top of Emily's head. "Are you remembering your wedding—and reliving the accident afterward?"

She nodded. "I felt blue earlier—when we were all ready and waiting to begin. My short-lived marriage was never happy. I was recalling how the ceremony marked the beginning of a long, tragic time for me. But all that sadness evaporated once I walked down the aisle ahead of Gina. Her happiness with Craig is undeniable. The love and energy all around us is palpable." She tipped her face up to his.

He pressed his lips to hers and they stayed like that until the server at Dragon Flame cleared his throat loudly to get their attention.

CHAPTER 38

M artha sat alone at her table, Garth snoring at her feet. Emily and Gina were dancing together to a Spice Girls song they'd played hundreds of times in Emily's bedroom. She smiled, remembering them both as young girls and as the fine women they'd grown into. Zoe and Diedre swirled and bobbed next to them.

Sylvia had sat with Martha before she'd taken herself off to find the ladies' room. They'd decided to have lunch the next time Martha was in the city. Sylvia had promised to email Martha an introduction to her book club and Martha was going to include Sylvia on her next visit to a gallery opening. She'd heard stories of people who'd met people at weddings—usually of the opposite sex. Martha was happy that she'd made a new friend in Sylvia; she had long ago given up hope of finding a new romantic interest.

She was pulled from her reverie when a tall, elegantly

dressed man with a shock of white hair approached and held out his hand to her. "I'm Doug Roberts. Gina's uncle."

Martha shook his hand and introduced herself. "I was wondering if you'd care to dance, but I see you have company." He gestured to Garth.

Martha flushed. It had been years—decades, even—since a man had asked her to dance. "I'm not sure Spice Girls is really my thing."

The song faded out and the old standard "Moon River" began to play.

"It's not mine, either. Fortunately, our DJ was open to suggestions."

"You requested this?"

"I figured it would increase my chances of success. But if you can't leave this guy…"

"Garth is the most well-trained dog on the planet," Martha said, getting to her feet. She commanded him to stay. "He'll be fine."

"We can step onto the floor right here, so we can keep an eye on him." Doug took her hand and steered her into his arms. They were soon waltzing in time to the music.

"You're a great dancer," Martha said.

"As are you."

"I'm rusty, I'm afraid."

"Nonsense. Dancing is like riding a bike—you never forget."

They gave themselves over to the pleasure of moving in the familiar pattern and didn't notice that they were soon alone on the floor. Guests gathered to watch, admiring the graceful couple. When the last strains of the song played, the crowd erupted in applause.

Doug stepped back, raising Martha's hand in the air, and nodded to the crowd.

Martha blushed and looked around herself in embarrassment.

The DJ spun "Bad Romance" and people piled back onto the dance floor.

Doug hung on to Martha's hand and raised an eyebrow.

She laughed, and they danced.

Grant and Emily soon appeared next to them, gyrating to the music. Grant leaned into Emily and put his lips to her ear. "Your mother and Gina's uncle were the couple that cleared the dance floor just now."

"Really?"

"Yes. They're still out here—and to be honest, they're putting us to shame."

"Mom and my dad loved to dance," Emily raised her voice to be heard.

"She looks like she's enjoying herself."

"I'm glad to hear it."

"Maybe we can get them to give us lessons. You're already a wonderful dancer. I'd like to learn. It'd be fun for us to command a dance floor the way they did."

The DJ continued to play tunes as the power from Craig's truck lived up to expectations. Servers cleared plates and glasses from the tables. The food trucks that Grant had engaged were packing up to leave. Everyone had commented on the quality—and originality—of the food. The cake had been cut, toasts made, and glasses raised.

Grant signaled to Zoe and Diedre. "The next song will be the last dance. It's time to pass these out to everyone and ask them to line up by the torches at the entrance to the garden," Grant said as they raced up to him.

"Yep. For the sparkler farewell. We know what to do," Diedre replied.

The girls set themselves to their task.

The DJ played "What a Wonderful World." Gina melted into Craig's arms as the wedding guests lined up on either side of the entrance. As the last verse of the familiar song played, Grant and Doug lit the sparklers.

Grant stepped into line with Emily while Doug joined Martha. The newlyweds ducked their heads and ran through the sparkler arch to a limousine waiting to whisk them away.

The wedding guests dispersed, but not before Doug had gotten Martha's phone number.

Martha gathered Zoe and Diedre. "I'll take these two upstairs with me," she said to Emily. "They're both ready to crash. I know I am. The two of you can take your time." She smiled at Grant.

"I'll bring the bouquet to our room," Zoe said to Emily. "It's neat that you caught it. That means you're the next to get married!"

"I don't think I deserve any credit for that," Emily replied. "Gina practically forced it into my hands."

"And I have the garter, Dad." Diedre twirled it in her fingers. "You definitely reached up to catch it."

"I can't spend one more second in these heels," Martha interjected. "Let's go, girls."

The three of them headed for their room.

"What a perfect night," Emily said. "I'm glad everything turned out like it did. And I'm very impressed with you and your brother. You saved the day, for sure."

Grant blew out a breath. "I'd be lying if I didn't say I'm very relieved. The company that runs both food trucks was my last shot. I don't know what I would have done if they'd have said 'no.'"

"We'd have ordered pizza and it would have been fine—but this was so much better."

He chuckled. "You're practical, aren't you? You're always going to find a solution."

"I guess that's me."

He turned to her. "One of the many things I love about you."

Garth stood and shook himself, then began walking around them, circling them with his leash.

Grant threw back his head and laughed. "This is what he did that first night we met—at Gina and Craig's engagement party."

"I remember," Emily said. "Like that scene in *101 Dalmatians*. Garth loves that movie."

Grant pulled her to him, and they melted into a deep kiss, with Garth at their feet.

CHAPTER 39

"I thought I'd beat you into the office," Emily said to Dhruv. "What in the world are you doing in this early?"

"How'd you know I was here?"

"Garth always takes me by your office when we go to get our coffee. I could hear you tapping away at your keyboard."

Dhruv continued to type. "I haven't been home. I've worked all night."

"Why in the world? Nothing we're doing is that urgent."

"I've been helping Denver on the cyber breach program."

"They're using our idea?"

"No. Another one. It's not as good."

Emily lowered herself into the chair beside his desk. "Dhruv—stop typing. Tell me what's going on."

Dhruv pulled his eyes away from his computer screen

and dropped his hands. "You know about the cyberattacks on our competitors?"

"Yes. You told me. But when I left the office on Wednesday, Denver hadn't contacted us."

"They did on Thursday. You were out and not checking your emails, so Kari contacted me."

Emily was silent, taking it all in.

"You remember Kari?"

"Of course I do. Does Ross Wilcox know you're helping with this?"

"I don't know. I don't care about him."

"You stayed all night working on this program that you say isn't as good as yours?"

"Yes. I worked all weekend on it. I'm finishing some programming now that I hope fixes it, but I don't think it will."

Emily pursed her lips. The one time she went off the grid and didn't check her emails, another division co-opted her best programmer. "I appreciate your dedication to the company, Dhruv. I'll make sure your efforts are noted in your personnel file. You'd better go home to get some rest. In fact, why don't you take the rest of the day off?"

"I'll go home as soon as I finish. I'm going to sleep until my flight to Denver."

"What?"

"Kari said they need me to come. My flight's at five fifteen. She emailed you."

Emily shot out of the chair. "I guess I'd better get to my emails."

"How was the wedding?" Dhruv asked.

"It was lovely."

"I'd like to hear all about it when I get back."

"Sure." Emily shook her head in disbelief. "Since when are you interested in weddings?"

Dhruv paused before he replied. "I just am."

"We'll talk about the wedding later, then. I'd like you back in the office before the end of the week. We have our own projects and responsibilities."

Dhruv had already resumed typing.

"Have a good trip." Emily made a beeline for her office. Company policy required Ross to have contacted her before he talked to one of her employees. She'd only been gone two days. Ross should have waited for her to return.

She plunked her coffee cup onto her desktop, sending some of the scalding liquid over the rim and onto her hand. She yelped and lunged for the tissue box that should have been on the right-hand corner of her desk.

Damn. The janitorial staff must have moved it when they cleaned over the weekend. Emily groped her desktop until she found her tissues. She snatched a wad from the box and sopped up the coffee.

Emily logged onto her computer and navigated to her inbox. She groaned when her screen reader informed her she had over two hundred messages waiting for her.

She'd first screen for messages from Ross, then she'd read those from Kari. Emily bristled when she thought of the nice young woman she'd met in Denver. Using Kari—another programmer at Dhruv's level—to sidestep company policy was a cheap move by Ross. Kari would only have been carrying out directions from her boss.

The first email from Ross on Thursday was written in an almost defiant tone. He'd acknowledged that, considering recent cyberattacks at competitors, they'd reviewed their programs and would implement modifications. He'd reiterated that the company was well protected.

By noon on Thursday, he'd emailed to ask if she had time for a conference call Friday morning. By mid-afternoon, he'd gotten back to her to see if she could speak to them Thursday afternoon. His tone had grown increasingly impatient, insinuating that she wasn't complying with company protocol to answer internal email promptly.

By Friday morning, he'd chastised her for not responding to his emails in a timely manner and informed her he'd be complying with company policy by having Kari reach out to Dhruv directly since Emily wouldn't respond to him.

She slapped the desk with her open palm. "What kind of idiot is this guy?" she asked Garth. "I had my out-of-office message on. He must not review his own email!"

She listened to half a dozen emails from Kari directed to Dhruv and copied to her. Kari had introduced herself and had apologized for going around Emily. She'd also laid out in careful detail the problems they were encountering with the Denver teams' current approach and solicited Dhruv's help. She'd reiterated that they all knew how crucial the programs to prevent cyberattacks were to the company.

Her last email had been a plea for Dhruv to come to Denver to help. Ross and Emily had been copied on it. Ross had forwarded it to Howard Kent and Howard had approved the trip.

Emily sank back against her chair. If Howard had approved it, there was nothing she could say.

She took a long drag on her now-cold coffee. If her team was going to be without Dhruv for who knew how long, she'd better get busy.

Emily picked up her cup and retraced her steps to the break room. They'll all be putting in longer hours than usual to program the next software update. The least she could do for herself was get a hot cup of coffee.

CHAPTER 40

"Stephanie's going to be alone this evening." Zoe looked over at Martha as Zoe set the table. "She and Dhruv always eat dinner together, but he's on his way to Denver."

"Emily called earlier this afternoon to tell me about Dhruv," Martha said. "She's working late tonight to cover for him in his absence."

"Can we invite Stephanie to eat with us?"

"What a good idea. I've made a big batch of spaghetti. We have plenty. Do you know her number?"

"It's in my phone." Zoe placed the call and Stephanie accepted the invitation. Zoe listened. "I'd love to help you order a dress for your birthday," Zoe replied. "Bring your laptop when you come for dinner."

Zoe turned to Martha, bouncing with excitement. "We're giving a surprise birthday party for Stephanie. Did Emily tell you?"

"She mentioned it, yes. You're having Mexican food. I offered to help."

"That's right. It's a milestone birthday. Thirty-five!" Zoe's eyes grew big. "That's when you're officially old."

Martha guffawed. "You're a kid at thirty-five. I'm not old, and I've seen way more birthdays than thirty-five."

Zoe looked stricken. "I'm sorry, Martha. I didn't mean..."

"I know you didn't." Martha patted Zoe on the back. "I'm glad we're having dinner with Stephanie. I'd like to get to know her better. Let's make sure we find out her favorite flavor of cake."

"For the party! That's a great idea."

A loud knock on the door announced Stephanie's arrival, along with her guide dog Biscuit.

Sabrina, now accustomed to the protocol around a dog wearing a working harness, greeted Biscuit politely and with uncharacteristic restraint.

Biscuit took Stephanie to the table, where she removed Biscuit's harness.

Sabrina approached Biscuit, and they were soon stretched out across the dog bed in the corner of the room.

Martha placed a large bowl of Caesar salad on the table, together with a loaf of garlic bread, fragrant and steaming hot, fresh from the oven. She served plates of spaghetti and handed them to Zoe to pass out.

"This smells wonderful," Stephanie said as Zoe put a plate in front of her. "Thank you so much for inviting me."

"Can I get you salad and bread?" Zoe asked.

"Thank you," Stephanie replied.

Zoe served her.

"Emily and Zoe have told me so much about you," Martha said, lowering herself into her chair. "I hear your birthday is coming up?"

"Yes. Dhruv and I," she cleared her throat and started again. "I'm sure Dhruv will take me somewhere nice for dinner. I thought I'd get a new dress."

"Great idea. A new dress always perks me up."

"I brought my laptop with me—maybe the two of you can help me select a few to order." Stephanie speared a fork full of salad.

"We'd love to," Martha said.

"How was the wedding?" Stephanie asked.

Martha recounted the weekend, including the ill-timed power outage and the impromptu change in the reception.

"What a shame, but it sounds like everyone pivoted quickly."

"They did. It turned out to be lots of fun. And you should have seen Zoe and her friend Diedre. They were so helpful." Martha took a bite of her garlic bread.

"That's the other junior bridesmaid?"

"Yep," Zoe said. "Junior bridesmaids are supposed to help people at the wedding and reception, so that's what we did." She told Stephanie about orchestrating illumination of the reception with cell phone flashlights until Craig's electric truck restored power to the lighting and the DJ.

"That was incredibly resourceful of you," Stephanie said. "I'm not surprised. Our Zoe is an intelligent, clever girl."

"That she is."

"What was your favorite part of the wedding, Zoe?"

Zoe opened her mouth, then paused. She cut her eyes to Martha before replying. "The wedding cake. It was so good."

"I love cake," Stephanie said. "What kind was it?"

"It was a carrot cake," Martha said. "I guess people do all kinds of wedding cakes these days."

"I've heard that. To tell you the truth, I'm not a fan. My very favorite cake in the entire world is a white cake with buttercream frosting." Stephanie replied. "I guess I'm boring."

Zoe's head whipped around to Martha and she dropped her fork, sending it clattering to the floor.

Martha put her finger to her lips to caution Zoe to remain quiet. "I'm with you on that. I love a traditional wedding cake."

Zoe got a clean fork and they finished the meal over talk of the unusually fine weather predicted for the next week.

"If you've finished your homework, Zoe, the two of you can start looking at dresses while I clean up the kitchen." Martha said.

"You did all the cooking. I'd like to help," Stephanie protested.

"Nonsense. I'm one of those cooks who cleans up as I go along, so all I need to do is load the dishwasher and wipe the counters. I'll be fine on my own."

"My homework is all done," Zoe said. "It was easy."

"Great. You can get started and I'll be with you in a jiffy."

~

STEPHANIE AND ZOE huddled together on the sofa while Martha moved about the kitchen at a leisurely pace.

"I've got six dresses in my shopping cart," Stephanie said. "Let me show you what I've picked so far." With the help of her screen reader, she navigated to her cart and turned the laptop toward Zoe.

Zoe scrolled through the images. When she was done, she leaned back against the sofa cushions.

"What do you think?" Stephanie asked. "Do you like any of them?"

"They're all long white dresses," Zoe said.

Stephanie quickly shut her laptop.

"Is that what you want?"

Stephanie remained quiet.

"They look like wedding dresses."

"I just thought... white would be nice."

"For your birthday?"

"White's not just for weddings," Stephanie replied.

"Why don't we look at some in blue?"

"Okay, sure. But don't remove the others from my cart."

"I won't," Zoe said. "Maybe some of them come in another color. I'll check." She opened the laptop and focused on the shopping cart page.

Stephanie bit her lower lip and waited.

"None of them are available in another color." She stared at Stephanie over the top of the screen. "The descriptions all say they're wedding dresses." Zoe popped up onto her knees on the sofa. You're getting married, aren't you? You and Dhruv are getting married!"

"Shhhhh…" Stephanie admonished, glancing toward the kitchen where Martha was running water.

"You are, aren't you?" Zoe persisted in a whisper.

"Yes."

"Are you having a big wedding? Like Gina?"

"No. Neither of us wants that. Indian weddings can be very elaborate and Dhruv can't deal with that. We thought we'd go to the courthouse to get married, but that would hurt both of our parents." She took a deep breath. "Can you keep a secret, Zoe?"

"Sure!"

"We're planning to get married at my birthday party."

"You mean the surprise one Emily and I are throwing for you?"

"Yes. Except I won't be the one who is surprised. It'll be all of you."

Zoe cupped her hand over her mouth to suppress a giggle. "That's the most fun thing I've ever heard of."

"We don't want a word of this to get out—to anyone. If it does, our families will try to get involved and it'll ruin everything."

"I understand." Zoe sank back onto her heels. "I can help you with all the details. After Gina's wedding, I know a bunch about them."

"I'm sure you do. Just remember, you can't tell anyone."

"I won't—you can count on me."

Stephanie nodded. "Now you know why I want a white dress. Which ones do you think will look good on me?"

"We should go shopping for your dress. It'll be like on *Say Yes to the Dress*. Do you know that show?"

"I've heard of it." Stephanie smiled and reached out to touch Zoe's hand. "Wedding dresses at shops have to be ordered months in advance. I don't have enough time for that."

"You can shop at Nordstrom. I'll go with you. They have a whole fancy dress department. I saw it when Diedre and I went there with Gina." Zoe leaned closer to Stephanie. "Can I tell Diedre? She can come with us."

"I don't want more people to know."

"Diedre and I can keep this a secret. I'll be a lot less likely to spill the beans if there's someone I can talk to about this. We'll be your wedding planners. And no one will suspect a thing."

"Well... it would be handy to have you know what we're planning. We'd talked about telling Emily."

"Don't. Diedre and I can handle this."

"Promise you'll tell me if it becomes too much," Stephanie said. "I can't let you get yourselves into trouble over this."

"I will—but it won't."

"What have you two found?" Martha asked as she turned off the kitchen light and stepped into the living room.

Stephanie slammed the laptop shut and both of them swung to face Martha.

"Nothing," Stephanie replied. "We decided none of the dresses I found would work."

"That's too bad. It's hard to order clothes online. I never have any luck."

"Can I go shopping with Stephanie? For her birthday dress?" Zoe asked.

"You'll have to ask Emily, but I don't know why not."

"Stephanie said I could ask Diedre to come along, too. We can go to Nordstrom."

"I can take us there on the bus," Stephanie said.

"If Diedre is joining you, I'll bet Grant would give you a ride."

"Let's go this Saturday," Zoe said. "Can we?"

"As Martha said, you need to ask Emily first." Stephanie said. "I'm free."

"Can I call Diedre?" Zoe asked Martha. "It's seven forty, and she's allowed to talk on the phone until eight."

"Go ahead," Martha replied.

"I'd better get going," Stephanie said. "I have papers to grade. Let me know about Saturday," she said as Zoe rushed off to call her friend.

Stephanie summoned Biscuit and put her into her harness. "Thank you for a delicious dinner, Martha."

"You're welcome here any time."

"Tell Zoe I'll see her in the morning to walk to school."

Martha shut the door behind her, glad that Emily had two wonderful friends in Gina and Stephanie.

"Is Zoe still up?" Emily asked as she and Garth entered the apartment.

"She's in bed, reading. She's excited to ask you something."

"Emily?" Zoe called from her room.

"What?" Emily hung her satchel by the door and removed Garth's harness.

"I need to talk to you," Zoe replied.

"I'll be right there, honey," Emily called.

"I'll feed this guy while you go see her. Are you hungry?" Martha asked. "We had spaghetti tonight. Want me to warm you up some leftovers?"

"That would be terrific," Emily said, traversing the familiar distance to Zoe's door. "I didn't have time for lunch and I'm starved." She stepped into Zoe's room.

Zoe scooted over, and Emily sat on the bed next to her. "Sorry I'm late. Dhruv's gone to Denver on business and I had a mountain of work to get through after being off for Gina's wedding."

"Stephanie told me about Dhruv when we were walking home from school. He's helping Denver on a big project."

"That's right."

"We had Stephanie over for dinner tonight, since she was going to be alone."

"I'm glad to hear it. She and Dhruv have gotten into a routine of eating all their meals together." Emily tucked the covers up around Zoe's chin. "They're like an old married couple."

Zoe's eyes bulged.

"We need to plan her birthday party. I'll have to bring work home every night this week, but maybe this weekend?"

"I wanted to ask you about Saturday. Can Diedre and I take Stephanie shopping for a new dress for her birthday?"

"I don't think that's a good idea. This is a surprise party. If you take her shopping, you'll give it away."

"She was already looking online for a new dress for her birthday. Stephanie thinks Dhruv is taking her to dinner at a fancy restaurant. She showed me the dresses in her shopping cart tonight."

"So she's buying one online?"

"No. None of them looked nice. Martha said it's hard to buy clothes online, so I offered to go with her to Nordstrom."

Emily chuckled. "You've become quite the Nordie's girl, haven't you?"

"You and Gina both say they're the best."

"I guess we do." Emily leaned back. "Does Stephanie want to go shopping with you?"

"Yes. And she said I could ask Diedre to go with us. I called her and she can go. Her dad will even drive all of us."

"I'll have to work at least half a day on Saturday."

"You're not invited," Zoe blurted out. "I mean—we knew you'd be too busy, so the three of us will go."

Emily remained silent.

"Please, Emily. Diedre and I are responsible, and we'll be safe with Stephanie."

"I know that. All right—you can go. I'll send you with money so you can buy lunch at the café. How about that?"

Zoe sprang up and threw her arms around Emily's shoulders.

"Okay, kiddo," Emily said, savoring the hug before releasing Zoe and turning out her light. "Time for you to go to sleep."

"Thank you, Emily. Night," Zoe replied as she burrowed into her pillow.

The aroma of her warmed-up dinner drew Emily to the kitchen counter.

"This smells great, Mom. Thank you."

"I gather you've had a rough day?"

Emily shrugged. "I wasn't expecting Dhruv to be out all week, but we'll get through it. I'm grateful that you stayed over tonight. I'll bring work home the rest of the week so I can be home for dinner with Zoe."

"About that," Martha said. "Would you mind if I stayed until Friday morning?"

"Of course not. What's changed your plans?"

"Sylvia asked if I wanted to join her for a lecture at the library on Wednesday afternoon."

"I knew the two of you connected at the wedding. I'm so glad for both of you. She seems very nice."

"I really like her. It'll be good to have a friend my age in the city."

"That's Wednesday?"

"Yes." Martha took a deep breath. "Doug Roberts has invited me to dinner Thursday night," she continued in a rush.

"Mom! You've got a date?"

"I don't know that I'd call it a date."

"Then what would you call it?"

"I'm not… It's just…" Martha stammered.

"I think it's a date and I couldn't be happier about it. He's a wonderful man. Gina thinks the world of him."

"You're okay with this?"

"Of course I am. You've been alone for a long time. I'd be thrilled for you to be in love again. Dad would want this for you," she concluded softly.

"That's a long way down the road, honey. All I'm doing is going out to dinner."

"And I, for one, am thrilled."

Emily opened her arms and Martha fell into them. The two women stood, swaying in their embrace.

"I think good things are coming to both of us, Mom."

CHAPTER 41

*R*oss Wilcox summoned his team to the conference room on Thursday afternoon. "I want to thank all of you for putting in long hours over the past ten days to revamp our security programs. You've worked incredibly hard, with singular focus. We've achieved our goal and I'm proud of you."

A collective sigh of relief went around the table as team members congratulated one another. Only one member of the team didn't join in.

"We couldn't have modified our program without Dhruv," Kari said.

"He should be here," chimed in another programmer.

"He's not on our group email list. I'll stop by to see him before he goes back to San Francisco," Ross said.

"He'll tell you he doesn't think our program is going to work," Kari said.

Ross swung to her, his brows knit in a straight line. "Our entire team thinks it will. Am I right?" He shifted his gaze from one person to the next as he went around the table.

One of the lead programmers spoke up. "We believe it will, but we may encounter recurring problems. Maintaining the integrity of the program will be a daily task."

"Then that's what we'll do."

The assembled team members avoided Ross's eyes.

"We can change this program as needed, can't we?"

The same lead programmer spoke again. "I'm not sure anyone here is as proficient—or as fast—as Dhruv."

Kari lifted her eyes from her lap and stared at Ross.

Ross sat back in his chair. "You're telling me we need to add to our team? We never replaced Tom when he retired last quarter, so I already have room in my budget."

"That's right," the lead programmer said, "and we want that new person to be Dhruv."

"I can take care of that right now," Ross said.

"You have to ask permission of his manager before you offer him a new position, don't you?" Kari blurted out.

"I'll handle Emily Main," Ross said curtly. "This program is mission critical to the company. Silly HR rules aren't going to get in the way. If we need Dhruv," he said, pushing his chair back from the table and standing, "we're going to have Dhruv."

DHRUV STOOD in Ross's doorway, shifting his weight from foot to foot.

"Come in." Ross stood from behind his desk and motioned Dhruv to a chair in front of it. "Please—sit down."

Dhruv hesitated, then sat.

"I'm sorry you weren't at our team meeting yesterday to celebrate the completion of our project."

"I'm not part of your team."

"That's one of the things I'd like to talk about, but first I want to congratulate you. I hear you handled the modifications that will guarantee the success of our program." Ross leaned across his desk and trained his most ingratiating smile on Dhruv. "I wanted to thank you, myself, personally."

"It won't work."

"I beg your pardon?" Ross pushed himself back into his chair.

"The modified program—hackers can get around it."

"I understand monitoring and modifications may be required, but my team says it works."

"They're wrong. It doesn't."

"So my entire team of programmers is wrong?"

"Yes."

"What do you think we should do?"

"Write the program I suggested."

Ross cracked his knuckles. "That's not an option, I'm afraid," he said, making a concerted effort to conceal his irritation.

"Then you'll have problems."

"My team tells me you know how to fix those problems."

"I do, but I'm not here."

"Which is the other reason I wanted to talk with you." He again leaned across the desk toward Dhruv. "I'd like to offer you a position on my team." Ross watched Dhruv closely, anticipating his excited and grateful response. When Dhruv remained silent, Ross continued. "As a lead programmer. This will be a promotion for you. You'll move up two pay bands, which will mean a significant salary increase. The company rarely bumps people two levels at a time, but I can make an exception for you."

Dhruv still didn't speak.

"I've checked your personnel file. You've had normal raises and bonuses, but it's been years since you've been promoted. This is a fabulous opportunity for you—one that I don't believe they can offer you in San Francisco." Ross raised both eyebrows as he tried to read Dhruv's thoughts.

Dhruv put his hands on his knees and thrust himself into a standing position. "No."

"What do you mean, no?"

"I'm not moving to Denver and taking a job on your team."

Ross's voice took on a steely edge. "This is a tremendous opportunity I'm offering you. You may never get another chance like this. Why don't you take some time to think about it?"

"I don't want the job." He walked to the door, then turned back. "Thank you. I should say thank you." He continued down the hallway.

"Stupid bastard," Ross muttered under his breath. "He can

rot in his little cubby in San Francisco for all I care. I never wanted him, anyway. We'll be fine as we are." He crumpled the offer letter he was going to slide across the desk to Dhruv and slammed it into the trash can under his desk.

CHAPTER 42

I knew Emily could use some extra sleep. We'd gotten to the office early all week long and had either stayed late or brought work home. We were both exhausted.

I'd stayed in my bed in the corner of her room until she'd gotten up to use the bathroom. I had to go, too. I seized the moment and intercepted her on her way back to bed.

"Do you need to go out, Garth?"

I lifted her hand with my nose.

"Okay," she said, shoving her feet into the slippers that were lined up against her nightstand and grabbing her phone. "We're coming straight back to bed as soon as you're done. I feel like I could sleep until noon."

She placed me in my harness, threw her jacket on over her pajamas, and we were outside in record time.

I knew I should be quick about my business.

Her phone pinged while I selected a spot that needed marking by me—one that bore too much Sugar and Rocco. I would correct that.

The screen reader informed her she had a text from Kari asking Emily to call her ASAP.

Emily swiped at her screen and was soon connected with Kari.

"What's up? Is there a problem with Dhruv?"

Kari sighed heavily. "Dhruv's been amazingly helpful. He's a genius, Emily."

"Your program was successfully modified?"

"Our folks seem to think so. Dhruv doesn't."

"Oh…"

"I think Dhruv's right."

"I'd put my money on him."

"Ross called us into a meeting—all of us except Dhruv—to congratulate us on our good work."

"That was nice."

"And I opened my big mouth and told him that Dhruv disagreed with us—that he said our program would fail."

"That was gutsy of you. I don't imagine Ross likes to be contradicted."

"No. He doesn't. He asked about it and one of our lead programmers told him our program would require daily monitoring and modification."

"That seems reasonable." Emily held her jacket closed against the morning fog. "This isn't why you want to talk, is it?"

"It's just that our programmer told Ross that Dhruv is the

only one capable of the necessary monitoring and modifications. He suggested we add Dhruv to our team." Her voice wavered.

"And you wanted to let me know Ross may try to poach Dhruv?"

"Exactly."

"That's decent of you, Kari. Ross hasn't emailed me the request form I need to approve before he offers a job to any of my employees. I wouldn't worry."

Even as Emily said the words, I could see her shoulders hunch and her lower lip twitch. She was worried.

"That's just it. I pointed that out to Ross in the meeting and he got a cat-that-ate-the-canary look on his face before saying he didn't have to comply with that policy because this is such a critical issue for the company."

Emily was now standing stock still, her rigid fingers pressing the phone against her ear.

"We already have an opening in our budget for a lead programmer. I believe Dhruv is at my level, so this would be a giant promotion and a huge salary increase."

Emily was silent.

"Are you still there?"

"Yes," came Emily's clipped reply.

"I thought about this overnight. I didn't want you to be blindsided."

"I'm glad you told me."

"You won't say anything to Ross about our conversation, will you? He's already pissed at me for speaking up at our team meeting. He can't know I called you."

"Of course I won't. I'm sure Ross can be very vindictive."

Kari didn't deny it.

"Has he made the offer to Dhruv?"

"I don't know. Dhruv was in Ross's office yesterday morning and headed to the airport as soon as he got out. I meant to catch him before he left the building, but I was in the ladies' room and in the two minutes I was in there, he'd gone."

"I'm outside with Garth. I'll check my email as soon as I get inside. Maybe Ross has done the right thing and notified me of his intentions."

"I hope so. Have you seen Dhruv since he got home?"

"Not yet. Thank you for filling me in. I appreciate your concern—and integrity."

"You're welcome. You would have done the same thing." Kari disconnected the call.

Emily jammed the phone into her pocket. "Did you hear that, Garth?"

I looked up at her and wagged my tail.

"That sniveling backstabber Ross Wilcox is going to offer Dhruv a job—hire him right out from under my nose!" A sniffle was followed by a sob and Emily was soon full out crying.

I sidled over to stand next to her.

"I shouldn't be crying about this, Garth. I'm being selfish and mean." She pinched the bridge of her nose to stem her tears. "It's just that Dhruv has been such an incredibly supportive friend to me. His concern and tenacity pulled me out of my dark depression right after I'd lost my vision.

Dhruv forced me to enroll at the Foundation for the Blind. I might never have gotten my life back on track—I might never have met you—if it hadn't been for him."

She had my attention now. Never met me? I couldn't bear to think about that.

"And here I am, being selfish. Thinking only of myself—my life and my team." She sank to one knee and buried her face in the fur around my neck. When she pulled away slightly, I swiped over her salty cheek with my tongue. "It sounds like Ross is offering Dhruv a huge promotion and a lot more money. Working on the company's cybersecurity team is very prestigious. He'll be recruited by other companies, too. I can't stand in his way. As much as I want to work with Dhruv for the rest of my career, I can't hold him back. If he wants this new job, I have to give my permission to Ross and my blessing to Dhruv."

The back door to the building creaked open behind us. I turned to see Sugar striding out the door, with Rocco prancing at her feet. Dhruv brought up the rear.

"Sugar?" Emily rose as Sugar joined us with her usual exuberant greeting.

"Hi, Emily," Dhruv said.

"Good morning. How was your trip?"

"Fine."

Emily waited, but Dhruv didn't elaborate.

"Did you fix the problem?"

"They think so. I don't."

"Huh…. So you just came home?"

"Yeah. I have work to do."

"Did Ross say anything to you?"

"He thanked me. He thinks I fixed the program. I didn't—not permanently. Hackers will break it."

Emily inhaled slowly. Sometimes talking to Dhruv was like getting blood out of a turnip. "Is that all Ross said to you?"

"Oh…. No."

"Well… what else did he say?"

"He offered me a job. A promotion."

"That's wonderful, Dhruv." She forced herself to continue. "You deserve every opportunity that comes your way. Aside from everything you've done for me personally, you're the most intuitive—"

"No."

"What?"

"I said 'no' to Ross. I don't want his job. I can't move to Denver."

I stepped even closer to Emily—I thought she was going to fall over.

"You turned it down?"

"Yes."

"And it was a lot more money?"

"It was."

"Didn't you like Denver?"

"I like Denver, but Stephanie is here. And my family. And you—and our team. This is home to me."

I felt a salty drop of water hit my nose. Emily was crying again, this time softly.

"You're crying. Why?"

"I'm so relieved that I'm not losing you, Dhruv." Her voice was thick with emotion. "Not just as an insanely talented employee, but as a dear friend. I wouldn't have stood in your way if it's what you wanted, but I'm glad you don't."

Dhruv had taken two steps back. I could tell Emily's show of emotion had triggered what humans call their fight-or-flight response.

"Okay... well... I've gotta go. See you around." Dhruv whistled for his dogs as he turned and sprinted up the steps and into the building.

Emily mopped at her eyes with the sleeve of her jacket. "I scared him off with all this blubbering, didn't I, Garth?"

I swung my tail from side to side.

"I'll tell you what," she said, her voice suddenly full of steely determination. "I'm going to find a way to give him that promotion and raise right here on my team. It's not in our budget, but I'll find a way."

She grasped my harness with a conviction that told me she wouldn't fail. When my Emily puts her mind to something, consider it done.

CHAPTER 43

"*Y*ou're sure about this, Stephanie?" Grant pulled over by the entrance to Nordstrom. "I can drop you three off here, go park in the garage, and meet you inside."

"No, Dad!" came the response from the back seat.

Stephanie chuckled. "I'm positive. They're doing me a favor. I hate shopping for clothes on my own."

"All right. Text me when you're ready to be picked up. I'm going to my office to catch up on paperwork—I'm only ten minutes away."

"This is so nice of you to ferry us both ways," Stephanie said as she opened her car door.

"Emily gave me money for lunch for all of us," Zoe said, "so it'll be a while." She and Diedre slid across the back seat and stepped onto the sidewalk next to Stephanie.

Biscuit was the last to emerge.

"Have fun," Grant said as Stephanie put Biscuit into her harness and Diedre shut the door.

"I gather you know where we're headed?" Stephanie asked.

"We do," the girls said in unison.

"It's called the special occasion dress department," Zoe said. "I looked it up online."

"Off you go. We'll follow," Stephanie said.

They set off for the second floor. Stephanie and Biscuit navigated the escalator like pros.

The department that featured fancy dresses was off to one side. Tall bars, hung with floor-length dresses, framed the area. Shorter racks with midi and knee-length dresses filled the center of the space. Satins reflected the high over-head halogen lights. Sequins sparkled. Lace dresses were available in pastel shades.

The three shoppers, plus Biscuit, stood at the entrance to the department.

"These are all so pretty. I can't wait until I'm old enough to shop in this department," Diedre said in a voice full of wonder.

"Are there any white dresses?" Stephanie asked.

Zoe and Diedre exchanged worried glances. The selection was slim. "There are a few," Zoe said. "We'll try them all on."

"Yes," Diedre chimed in. "That's what Gina had us do when we bought our junior bridesmaid dresses."

A salesclerk approached them. "You ladies look like you're on a mission," she said, smiling broadly as she took in the four of them. "How can I help?"

"I'm getting married and I need a dress," Stephanie said.

"Congratulations! We don't stock wedding dresses in the store anymore, but I can help you select one online. We can receive it here in the store and you can come in for alterations. When's the big day?"

"Three weeks from today," Stephanie replied.

"Ahh...," the salesclerk gasped. "That soon."

"I know I don't have time to order a real wedding dress," Stephanie said. "I just thought... I mean I don't really need a wedding dress." Stephanie began to back out of the department.

"Yes, you do," Zoe insisted. "That's why we came here." She looked at the salesclerk. "We know you'll help us find the perfect dress for Stephanie. My grandma and I watched that show on TV—from that New York bridal store. They said every bride needs their perfect dress."

"They're exactly right," the clerk agreed. "We're going to find your dress. Why don't I put you in our largest fitting room and you can tell me what you're looking for?"

The entourage followed the clerk through the department to the fitting rooms. They passed a mirrored alcove with a raised platform flanked by chairs. The clerk continued to the last fitting room on the right and unlocked the large room, which had a chair and a full-length, three-way mirror.

"I'll bring two more chairs," the clerk said.

"No," Zoe said. "We'll wait for Stephanie to come out to that raised thingy." She gestured to the alcove that they'd just passed. "That's how they do it on the show. You bring her out and turn her toward us and we tell her what we think."

The clerk chuckled. "You're quite right. That's exactly how it's done on *Say Yes to the Dress*."

"You watch the show?" Stephanie asked.

"Doesn't everyone? Now—what are your thoughts about your dress?"

"I know I want a white dress. I'm pretty traditional."

"When and where are the ceremony and reception?"

Stephanie filled her in on the details.

The clerk clasped her hands together and brought them to her chest. "That's so romantic. I love it. Do you want a long dress—with a train?"

Stephanie shook her head no. "I'll be with Biscuit. I don't want anything we could trip over."

"Got it. Why don't you have a seat here? The girls can go to the alcove. I'll bring you all water bottles and then I'll pull dresses for you to try. They won't all be in your size. Just remember, we can alter anything."

Stephanie and Biscuit sat in the fitting room as the girls followed the salesclerk to the alcove.

The clerk was back with water bottles in a flash and soon returned with an armful of dresses.

"These are in varying shades of pure white to cream," she said. "Let me help you into the first one."

The dress was a chic satin sheath two sizes too big. The clerk pinched the extra fabric in the back with clamps designed for the purpose. Its hem dragged on the ground. "What do you think?"

Stephanie ran her hands over the sleek fabric. "I don't think it feels like me," she said. "It's too modern—and sexy."

"You've got a wonderful figure and you are sexy, but it is a modern silhouette. Shall we show the girls?"

"This dress isn't it. I don't want to waste your time."

"Don't you worry about me." The salesclerk was firm. "I've got all day to spend with you. Those sweet girls are so excited and have been waiting very patiently. I think we'd better get you out there."

Stephanie chuckled. "They're really something, aren't they?"

"Absolutely."

"Alright. Let's go."

"I'm going to walk behind you, holding up the hem. You and..."

"Biscuit."

"You and Biscuit lead the way."

Stephanie stood on the elevated platform and turned this way and that, as directed by Zoe.

"That dress looks like Emily," Zoe said. "Not you."

"I agree," Diedre said. "It needs to be more girly."

"That's what I thought," Stephanie said.

"We've got several more," the clerk said. "Are you girls doing okay?"

"We are," they chorused.

Stephanie, Biscuit, and the clerk made four more trips to the alcove. They rejected another satin dress and two that were heavy with sequins. The last dress was a knee-length lace with a trim bodice and full skirt.

Stephanie stood on the platform, running her hands along the sides of the dress. "It feels like it fits."

The salesclerk picked up the shoulders. "I'd suggest we add a thin shoulder pad, but it's your size and doesn't need alteration."

"What do you think?" Stephanie turned to Zoe and Diedre. "This is the last one." Her voice sounded pleading.

"It's nice," Diedre said. "You look very pretty."

"It's appropriate for a casual afternoon wedding," the clerk said.

"It's just that it's not very bride-y." Zoe couldn't hide her disappointment. "Anyone could be wearing this dress."

"I don't really care about looking like a bride. This is our last choice. I just want to get a dress and go home."

"No!" the clerk said, startling all three of the shoppers. "This is not what I want for you. You need to have your 'say yes' moment."

"But we're out of dresses."

"Can you give me a bit more time? I want to scour every inch of this store—look at every sale rack and all the dresses that have been returned and are waiting to go back out on the floor. I'll put this dress on hold for you," she touched the skirt of the dress that Stephanie was wearing, "but I think your perfect dress is in this store. We just haven't found it yet."

Biscuit hopped to her feet and emitted a soft "woof."

The clerk laughed. "You see? She agrees with me."

"It's just after eleven," Zoe said. "We could eat lunch and come back."

"Yes! That'll give me enough time. I'll be waiting for you when you return."

The three shoppers headed for the in-store restaurant while the clerk attacked her mission like a heat-seeking missile.

Stephanie and the girls tried to enjoy a leisurely lunch, but they were all eager to see what the clerk had found.

"I don't want any of us to be disappointed if we come home with that last dress I tried on. It'll be just fine."

"You looked very pretty in it," Diedre said, shooting a warning glance at Zoe.

Zoe shrugged, but remained silent.

The clerk was waiting for them when they returned to the special occasion dress department. Her ear-to-ear smile told Zoe what she'd wanted to know.

"I only found one more dress, but I think it'll be 'the one.' " She led them back to the fitting room. "It's out of season and was on the rack waiting to go to a Nordstrom Rack store. I talked to the store manager and I can give you a steep discount."

The girls took their seats in the mirrored alcove.

Stephanie followed the clerk to the fitting room and stepped out of her T-shirt and jeans.

"It's a winter white cut velvet, with the most beautiful seed pearl work on the bodice and at the cuffs. It's an A-line silhouette." She helped Stephanie into the dress and zipped the back. "Oh," the clerk uttered in satisfied tones, "the fit is perfect. The waist hits you correctly and the ankle length is… regal."

Stephanie touched the beading along the princess neckline and down the front of the bodice. "I love this. I can feel that it's pretty."

"The cut velvet has an excellent drape to it." The clerk stood back. "I wouldn't change a thing."

"Do I look like a bride?" Stephanie's voice was thick with emotion.

"You most certainly do! You wouldn't need a veil, either. Put that gorgeous blonde hair of yours up in a clip with pearls on it, and you'll be all set."

"I've already made an appointment to get my hair done that day. The girls can help me buy a clip."

"Shall we go out and show them the dress?"

Stephanie nodded. She and Biscuit made their way to the alcove, the salesclerk trailing behind.

Before Stephanie stepped up on the platform, both girls were squirming in their chairs with excitement.

"Well?" Stephanie asked, turning to them.

"I love it!" Zoe cried.

"So beautiful," Diedre added.

"You look like a bride!" Zoe jumped out of her chair. "Are you ready to say it?"

"What?" Stephanie asked.

"Are you saying 'yes' to the dress?" Zoe asked.

Stephanie's smile outshone the halogens. "YES!"

Zoe and Diedre rushed to Stephanie's side, and she drew them to her in a group hug.

The clerk pulled a tissue from her pocket and dabbed at her eyes.

"I hope you come back and show me pictures of your wedding."

"I will," Stephanie assured her. "Thank you so much for going the extra mile and finding my dress for me."

"You three—four—have made my day," the clerk said. "Now, let's get you back into your clothes while I see if my manager will approve an extra ten percent off."

CHAPTER 44

*M*y tail slapped the floor of its own accord. When Dhruv was close by, I couldn't control it. *What was that word humans used? Namaste?* The goodness in me recognized the goodness in Dhruv.

"Hey, Dhruv. I was checking in with Emily after my vacation." Dhruv's coworker, Rhonda, stood in Emily's doorway, nursing a cup of coffee. "Sounds like I missed a lot."

"That's an understatement," Emily said. "But we survived. I'm glad you're back, however."

"I'd better go tackle my inbox," Rhonda said. "She's all yours, Dhruv."

"I was looking for *you*, Rhonda," Dhruv replied.

"Really? What can I help you with?"

"Not here."

Rhonda took a step back. "Oh... okay."

"It'll only take a minute."

"In that case," Emily said, "you can stay right where you are. I'm going to the ladies' room." She picked up her cane. "I'll leave Garth here. I can tell he wants his morning belly rub from Dhruv."

I forced my tail to be still. She was correct—I wanted Dhruv's attention. He was a master belly-rubber. But I would never abandon my duty to Emily. I got to my feet and inched my way out from my usual spot under Emily's desk.

"It's fine, Garth," Emily said as she sailed past me. "I can go down the hall and come back on my own."

Dhruv lowered a hand to me.

I sniffed it and gave him a lick before lying down and rolling onto my back.

Dhruv squatted next to me and began sweeping his hands across my belly in concentric circles. "Will you marry me?"

Rhonda choked on a sip of her coffee. "What?" she croaked.

"I'm getting married and we need someone to perform the ceremony. I remember you officiated at your nephew's wedding. So—would you marry me?"

"Dhruv! Congratulations! I hadn't heard."

"It's a secret. Nobody knows."

"You'd better tell me more."

Dhruv gave a succinct account of the planned surprise wedding. "What do you think?"

"It sounds lovely, Dhruv. You've thought of a solution that should satisfy everyone." She blinked rapidly. "I'm beyond thrilled to hear this. You're such a kind, dear man... you deserve..."

"She'll be back any minute," Dhruv interrupted her. "Will you do it?"

"I'd be honored."

"Thank you."

"I'll need to talk to you and Stephanie about your ceremony."

"Sure."

"And you've got your marriage license?"

"Yes. We're all set."

"Let's get together—the three of us—to plan the ceremony. Is there anything else I can do to help?"

"Nope."

"And Emily doesn't know? Even though she's throwing the birthday party?"

"The only other people who know besides Stephanie and me are Zoe and Diedre."

"That's what you said—two fourth graders." She cocked one eyebrow at him.

Dhruv continued to rub my belly. "That's right. They're helping with everything."

"That's a lot of responsibility for them."

"They've done weddings before."

Rhonda chuckled. "Give them my phone number. If they need anything—anything at all—tell them to call me."

"I will—but they won't."

"I'd give you the most enormous hug, but I can hear Emily coming."

Dhruv shot to his feet and stepped back, out of her reach.

He blew out a big breath, swinging his arms at his sides. "That's a relief!"

"Are you relieved because I won't hug you, or because I can perform the ceremony?" Rhonda chided.

"Both. Mainly I'm happy that we're all set. Thank you." He quickly left Emily's office.

Rhonda and I watched him go. "I don't like keeping secrets, boy," she said to me, "but this is a special case." She headed to her office.

I had to agree with her. I settled down to wait for Emily. This Monday morning was off to a good start.

CHAPTER 45

*E*mily's phone announced that Howard Kent was calling.

She sat forward in her desk chair and filled her lungs with a calming breath before answering. When she'd emailed him the day before, asking him to call her at his convenience, she'd known what she wanted to say to him. Now that he was on the line, she wasn't so sure.

"Hello, Howard," she said, forcing an even tone. "Thank you for calling."

"I meant to get back to you after your Denver trip. Time just slipped away from me. I understand that you and Dhruv helped get everything fixed. Well done! I love to see that sort of interdepartmental cooperation."

She bit her lip while she formulated her response. "I don't agree that our systems have been fixed," she said in clipped tones.

"Ross reported that they'd detected a few minor errors in our programs to fight cyberattacks, but that they'd all been resolved. He said that programmer of yours…" Howard paused, searching his memory for the name.

"Dhruv," Emily supplied.

"Thank you—Dhruv—had been extremely helpful."

"Did you know he tried to hire Dhruv—to get him to move to Denver to join his team?"

"I don't get involved in personnel moves at that level. I'm assuming Ross got your approval before he offered Dhruv the job?"

"He did not." Emily's voice was icy. "That's why I asked you to call. I don't appreciate Ross doing an end run around me."

"There must have been some sort of miscommunication —manager approvals are a well-established company protocol. What did Ross say when you talked to him?"

"I didn't," Emily said. "Dhruv wasn't interested in the job, so it was a moot point."

"Except now you feel like Ross went behind your back. Don't you think you should clear the air with him? After all —you and Dhruv were key players in correcting the problems."

Emily sucked in another deep breath. "Dhruv and I don't think the problem has been solved. As Dhruv told the Denver team, he's bought them some time. That's all."

Howard was silent for a moment before he continued. "How long?"

"A few weeks—maybe several months. But a breach of our systems is going to happen."

"It's already been more than a few weeks since either of you has been there. Maybe Ross is correct, and the system now works. It is his area of expertise, after all."

"We'll know soon enough."

"Ross doesn't report to me, so I'd have to take any complaint to his manager. Since you haven't even contacted Ross to hear his side of the story, I'm hesitant to start down that road."

"I understand," Emily said stiffly.

"So you'll talk to Ross and let me know if you're still not satisfied with his reasoning and want to file a formal complaint against him?"

"If I want you to take this matter any further, I'll call Ross first." Emily pursed her lips. There was no way she was going to listen to Ross spew made-up justifications of his actions.

"Great." Howard's voice dripped with relief. "And, again, I'm grateful that both you and Dhruv assisted another department. I'll make sure your files are noted with your willingness to collaborate with other teams."

"Thank you," Emily said.

"My pleasure. Call anytime," Howard said before ending the call.

CHAPTER 46

"*O*ur daughters are seeing more of each other than we are," Grant commented. He put his feet up on the ottoman and laid his phone on the arm of his favorite chair.

Emily chuckled. "Neither of them is crazy busy with jobs, like we are." She slipped her AirPods into her ears and sunk back against her pillows. "I like that we talk every evening at bedtime. I look forward to it."

"Me, too," Grant said, "but I want to be with you." He sighed heavily. "I'm afraid it won't be this weekend. My mom can't babysit—she's going on a cruise with some of her book club buddies."

"Good for her," Emily said. "My mom isn't available, either. She and Doug are going out again. Dinner and dancing."

"They go out two or three times a week, don't they?"

"Yep. She keeps telling me they're just good friends—that they're not serious—but I'm not so sure. She's as giddy as a schoolgirl when she talks about him."

"To paraphrase what you just said—good for them."

"Why don't you and Diedre come here for dinner Saturday night? I'm sure the girls will want to hang out together this weekend. We can order pizza and have a movie night."

"If it puts me in the same room with you, I'm in. I'll bring the pizza."

"And I'll get a big bag of popcorn." She stifled a yawn.

"Burning the candle at both ends?"

"I'm afraid so." She yawned again. "Sorry. It's not you."

"I hope not."

"I'm excited to see you this weekend. With any luck, we'll have a few minutes alone."

"You mean we'll make out like teenagers while our daughters are in Zoe's bedroom?"

Emily chuckled. "You know very well we won't do that."

"Still—it's nice to dream. And speaking of dreams, I'm going to let you get some sleep."

"Thanks. Talk to you tomorrow. Sweet dreams." Emily disconnected the call. She burrowed into her pillows and was soon asleep.

EMILY SLID the remaining two slices of pizza into ziplock bags and placed them in the refrigerator.

Sabrina was sniffing the floor under the table, hoping to hoover up any crumbs that had been dropped. I didn't engage in such undignified behavior. If the occasional table scrap did land on the ground, I would be courteous enough to deal with it, but I wasn't constantly on the prowl for scraps like Sabrina.

"What do you girls want to watch?" Grant called from the living room. "Shall we look for something on the Disney channel?"

My ears perked up. I loved the Disney channel. Especially *101 Dalmatians*. That was my favorite movie of all time.

I got out of my bed and padded to the living room. If they were watching Disney, I would join them.

"We can't watch TV with you guys," Zoe said.

"What do you mean?" Emily asked.

"We're going to Dhruv and Stephanie's," Zoe said. "Both of us."

"They won't want to spend their Saturday night with you—"

"They do!" Zoe interrupted. "They invited both of us." She cut her eyes to Diedre.

"We're having a scrabble tournament," Diedre quickly supplied.

"Do you even know how to play Scrabble, honey?" Grant asked his daughter.

"Zoe's been teaching me," came the fast reply.

"I have," Zoe said. "And we'd better get going. We don't wanna be late."

"All right," Emily said. "But don't overstay your welcome."

The girls looked at each other.

"What does that mean?" Zoe asked.

"If it looks like they're getting tired, you need to come home. Text me first so I can watch you walk down the hall."

"We will," Zoe said.

"Why don't the two of you go somewhere? Like on a date or something?" Diedre suggested.

"That's a great idea," Zoe exclaimed. "We'll be fine with Stephanie and Dhruv."

"I don't think it would be fair to them for us to just leave." Grant said. "We'll stay here and watch a movie, as planned."

"Watch a long movie, okay?" Zoe said. "Scrabble tournaments take time." She opened the door and the two girls walked down the hall.

Dhruv opened his door. "Got 'em," he called to Emily, as the girls entered his apartment.

Emily closed her door, and Grant swept her into his arms.

"I guess we'll get that alone time, after all."

They stood, entwined in each other's arms, and kissed.

The television screen remained dark. I was about to return to my bed in the corner of the living room when Emily and Grant forced themselves apart.

"We'd better not. The girls are right down the hall," Emily said reluctantly.

"I agree." Grant was breathing hard.

"Let's watch that movie."

They moved to the sofa and sank down next to each other.

"What sounds good?" Grant asked.

"I think we watch enough Disney with the girls. I've never seen *La La Land*," Emily said. "It's supposed to have wonderful audio description for the visually impaired."

"Brilliant suggestion. I haven't seen it, either." Grant found the movie on Emily's streaming service.

The screen filled with cars on a freeway and lots of people dancing. I was intrigued and made my way to the sofa, settling at Emily's feet.

The movie continued, and the opening credits appeared on the screen. My eyelids grew heavy. By the time the movie was done, Grant, Emily, and I were sound asleep.

ZOE AND DIEDRE rushed past Dhruv to find Stephanie waiting for them in the living room.

She held out her arms to them, and they fell into her. "Did your parents suspect anything?"

"Nope. They think we're playing Scrabble."

"Good," Stephanie said. "Dhruv, this is Grant's daughter, Diedre."

"Hi. Stephanie said you were a big help with her dress. Thank you for keeping our secret."

"This is the coolest thing ever!" Diedre said.

"Okay," Zoe said, pulling a piece of paper from her pocket. "I've made a list of what we need to do."

"That's very efficient of you," Stephanie said.

"It's what wedding planners do," Zoe said. "I've been

researching online. So..." She unfolded the paper and smoothed it out on the coffee table. "The bride has her dress."

"Have you bought clips for your hair—like the salesclerk suggested?" Diedre asked.

"I've got three of them in my online shopping cart," Stephanie said. "I thought you girls could help me decide which one to order."

"We'd love to!" Diedre clapped her hands together.

"Let's get through the list first," Zoe said. "What about you, Dhruv? What are you wearing?"

"I have a navy blue sherwani that I wear to weddings. I'll wear it."

"Don't you want a new one?"

"No. It's fine."

"Clothes are all set." She made a check mark on her list. "Emily also ordered food online last week. She said we'll have sodas and snacks too. From the grocery."

"What about a cake?" Dhruv asked.

"Emily ordered a birthday cake from the bakery on the corner." Zoe pulled another paper from her pocket. "This is the confirmation email. It's got an order number on it." She held the paper out to Dhruv. "Can you call them to change it to a wedding cake? I'd do it, but I sound like a kid. I don't think they'll make the change if I call."

"I'm not sure what to ask them to do."

"Why don't we call them together, Zoe, on Monday after school," Stephanie said.

Zoe scribbled a note on her list. "Good idea. I knew you

like white cake and buttercream icing, so that's what we ordered," Zoe said. "We just need them to make it look like a wedding cake and not say 'Happy Birthday, Stephanie.' That's what Emily ordered."

"Great attention to detail," Stephanie said.

"Zoe and I are going to push the sofa against the wall in their living room and put up chairs," Diedre said.

"There's gonna be twelve other people, and then the two of you, obviously," Zoe said.

"Plus the person who does the marrying part. Like a pastor," Diedre added.

"That'll be Rhonda. She's one of my co-workers. In fact, she asked me to give you her phone number in case you need any help. I'll send it to Zoe."

"We've got six chairs at our apartment," Zoe said. "Can we borrow your dining room chairs?" She looked at Dhruv.

"Sure. How are you going to keep things secret if you're setting up chairs and you have a wedding cake delivered instead of a birthday cake?" Dhruv asked.

"We've figured it all out," Diedre said. "Zoe will keep Emily busy in the kitchen with the food and snacks, and I'll arrange the chairs."

"Emily will hear you moving chairs in the living room, but that shouldn't be a problem. She won't be able to tell if the cake says 'Happy Birthday'—or not," Stephanie said.

"We're meeting with Rhonda this week to go over the final details of the ceremony. She'll arrive with the other guests at four and will take charge of announcing the wedding," Dhruv said.

"This is going to work!" Stephanie turned to Dhruv, and he swept her into his arms.

Zoe and Diedre stood, arms crossed over their chests, watching them.

"All you have to do is order your hair clip and we're all set," Zoe added.

"I'll set up the Scrabble board while you do that," Dhruv said.

The four of them were deep into a cutthroat game when Grant and Emily eventually knocked on Dhruv's door, saying it was time for the girls to come home.

CHAPTER 47

"*C*an I come with you, Martha?" Zoe asked.

"Sylvia invited me to the book club luncheon she's hosting at her home," Martha said, putting her hand on Zoe's shoulder and smoothing her hair off her forehead. "I can't just bring you along. I'd say we could have dinner together tonight, but I'm seeing Doug. How about we make blueberry pancakes tomorrow morning? They're your favorite."

"But Diedre's going to be there this weekend because her dad is out of town at a conference. She's invited me over there to spend the night. Her grandma said it's fine."

"I didn't realize Sylvia was taking care of her grand-daughter. I'm sure Sylvia would be happy for Diedre to have a friend over. Is it all right with you, Emily?"

Emily brought her head up from her laptop at the sound

of her name. "That's fine by me. I'm still playing catch-up at work."

"Promise me you won't spend your entire Saturday hunched over your computer," Martha said.

"I won't. I'm getting a haircut at two."

"Do you need a ride?"

"It's a nice day, and it's less than a mile away. Garth will enjoy the walk. We'll be fine."

"Have you got your stuff ready?" Martha asked Zoe.

Zoe held up her backpack. "Right here."

Martha crossed to where Emily sat at the kitchen island, her laptop open in front of her. She planted a kiss on the top of her daughter's head. "Enjoy a day on your own. I'll be back before Doug picks me up at six."

"Be a good girl for Mrs. Johnson." Emily stood and held out her arms to Zoe.

"I will." Zoe and Emily hugged.

"And have fun," Emily said as Zoe followed Martha out the door. She returned her attention to the report she'd been working on.

Martha made the short drive to Sylvia's townhome. She found a parking spot along the street on the next block. She pulled the hostess gift from the back seat. Martha hoped Sylvia would enjoy the bottle of lemon strawberry hand lotion as much as she did—it was one of her favorite indulgences. The two started walking.

Diedre was waiting for them on the front steps.

The two girls ran to each other and threw their arms around each other's neck.

Martha grinned, remembering similar scenes between Gina and Emily many years earlier.

"Gramma told me to bring you to the back patio," Diedre said to Martha. "That's where her book club always meets." She turned and led them through the house.

Sylvia rose to greet Martha. "This is the woman I've been telling you all about," she said to the group milling around the patio. "Let me introduce you to everyone."

"Let's go," Diedre said to Zoe. "Wait till you see what I found!"

The two girls tore back into the house.

"What?"

Diedre bounded up the stairs to the second floor. "My room's at the front of the house," she said. "You can put your backpack in there."

Diedre entered a small room painted in soft pink that barely accommodated two twin beds, separated by a nightstand, and a small dresser that sat under a window overlooking the street. White eyelet curtains framed the window and duvets covered in floral fabric featuring peonies in shades ranging from blush to deep magenta sat below mounds of pillows. A high shelf housing a menagerie of stuffed animals ran around the room.

"That's your bed," Diedre said, pointing to the one closest to the door.

"This is so pretty!" Zoe set her backpack on the floor next to her bed. She turned around slowly, examining the room. Her head came up suddenly, and she pointed toward the middle of the shelf. "I have that exact same cat and the walrus, too."

"Really?"

The girls looked at each other and giggled.

"I've also got a playroom on the third floor," Diedre said.

"There's a third floor? I've never been in a house with more than two floors."

Diedre nodded. "Come on. What I want to show you is up there." She took Zoe to an alcove at the far end of the hallway, where a narrow, twisted staircase led to the upper floor.

The girls scrambled to the top.

A wood paneled room with a low ceiling ran the length of the house. Windows sat in dormers at the front and back of the room. Light filled the space on the sunny day. Over-stuffed bookcases lined one wall while labeled plastic totes were stacked against the opposite wall. A child's table and four chairs stood in the middle of the room. A plastic tote sat on the table, its lid discarded on the floor.

"That's one of my dress-up boxes," Diedre said.

"I loved playing dress-up when I was little," Zoe said.

"Me, too." Diedre reached into the open box and pulled out a bridal veil. "I loved my bride dress. I wore it until it fell apart. Gramma finally threw it away. This is all that's left of it."

Zoe took the well-worn veil from Diedre and turned it over in her hands, stopping at a large tear in the tulle.

"I think we should use this for the wedding," Diedre said.

Zoe raised her eyes to Diedre. "This isn't... Stephanie already bought those fancy hair clips."

"Not for Stephanie," Diedre said. "For Biscuit."

A smile slashed across Zoe's face. "Of course! I forgot all about Biscuit."

"I know it's torn, but I think we can cut off the torn part and glue some flowers or pearls to it." She pointed behind her to a row of totes labeled *Craft Supplies*. "I've got tons of stuff here we can use. We'll attach it to a headband that will fit behind Biscuit's ears. Gramma's going to be busy with her book club for hours. We can get it all done and in your backpack before she knows what we're up to."

"This is a great idea! Biscuit has to be a bride, too."

"We've got a plan. I'm starving. Are you?" Diedre lifted her eyes to Zoe.

Zoe nodded.

"Gramma said we could help ourselves to food. She's got a buffet set up in the kitchen. Let's go get our plates and bring them up here."

"Sure. We can eat while we work."

The girls shared a conspiratorial smile and raced down the two flights of stairs to the kitchen.

"It's quiche," Diedre said, scrunching up her nose. "Gramma says ladies like it."

"You said it's egg, cheese, and spinach pie? I don't think so," Zoe said.

"There's a big tray of fruit," Diedre said, pointing to the end of the kitchen island. "And a bunch of different kinds of muffins. I ate banana ones this morning. They're really good. Plus, we've got cookies."

Diedre peeked out the French doors leading to the patio. "Gramma's friends are all eating. We can take what we want."

The girls scooped the remaining watermelon, strawberries, and grapes from the fruit tray onto a plate. They put two muffins on another plate and balanced four large, iced sugar cookies on top.

"We can each put a water bottle in our pocket," Zoe said.

"Good thinking," Diedre replied, handing a water bottle to Zoe and tucking one in her pocket. "Let's go. We've got work to do."

The girls set their food on one corner of the table in the playroom and got busy with their task. They nibbled as they worked, and by the time their plates were empty, they were done. A bridal veil with a flowered headpiece, suitable for a yellow lab, lay in the center of the table.

"That headband you found should fit Biscuit," Zoe said.

Diedre nodded in satisfaction. "She'll look so cute. I can't wait to tell Stephanie."

Zoe snapped her fingers. "I've got a better idea. This can be a surprise for Stephanie and Dhruv! They think they're doing all the surprising, but this way we'll have something that they won't know about."

"I like it!" The girls high-fived.

"There's only one more thing on the list that we don't have," Zoe said.

"A bridal bouquet," Diedre said.

Zoe nodded. "And a garter."

"Stephanie said she doesn't care about having flowers," Diedre said, "but I want her to have them."

"Me too!"

"Are you hoping for what I'm hoping for?"

"That Emily catches the bouquet and your dad catches the garter?"

"Yep. Like at Gina and Craig's wedding." She grew serious and looked at Zoe. "Would you be okay with them getting married?"

"Are you kidding? Of course I would!"

"Then we'd be actual sisters—step sisters!"

"Do you think catching the bouquet and the garter really works?" Zoe asked.

"To make people be the next to get married? I don't know. But I think we should try to make it happen."

Zoe nodded. "I agree."

"I have some old, stretched out hair scrunchies in here. I'm sure I have a blue one," Diedre said. "We can tie a bow on it and use that for the garter."

"That works." Zoe pursed her lips. "I want Stephanie to have a bouquet with real flowers."

"I could pick some from Gramma's garden," Diedre said. "We don't have flowers at our house."

"They need to be a kind of flower that Stephanie can smell."

"That's right. Gramma is always complaining that roses

from the grocery store look good but don't smell like anything."

"How are we going to get a bouquet of pretty smelling flowers?"

Zoe raised an eyebrow. "We can call the lady who's going to perform the ceremony. She said we could call her if we need help. Dhruv gave me her name and number."

"Yeah! Let's get back to my room with Biscuit's veil before Gramma and Martha come looking for us." She carefully folded the veil around the headpiece and they made their way to Diedre's room.

Zoe retrieved her phone from her backpack. "Let's search for 'good smelling flowers for a bridal bouquet.' " She tapped at her screen and scrolled. "It says hyacinth, lilac, lavender, magnolia, freesia, gardenia, and peony blossoms are all good. Some are more expensive than others. Not all of them are available all year long." She looked up at Diedre.

"I've saved up twenty-five dollars from my allowance, so we've got money."

"Wow! That's awesome."

"Let's call this lady. Maybe she knows a good place to buy a bridal bouquet."

"We'll give her our list of nice-smelling flowers."

"Right. And I can hand her my money at the party."

Zoe tapped at the screen of her phone and scrolled. "Here she is—her name is Rhonda."

The girls looked at each other and nodded.

Zoe made the call and put her phone on speaker.

Rhonda answered the call from the local area code but unknown number.

"This is Zoe and Diedre. We're Stephanie and Dhruv's," she hesitated before continuing, "wedding helpers."

"I was hoping you'd call." Rhonda's voice was warm. "Dhruv's told me all about you and what a grown-up, wonderful job the two of you are doing."

The girls pressed their heads together, their grins melting into each other.

"Is there something I can help with? I'd really like to."

"Stephanie needs a bouquet," Zoe said. "She said she doesn't want one, but we don't believe her."

"Quite right," Rhonda said. "Every bride needs a bouquet."

"We need flowers that smell good. We researched the best ones." Zoe read the list to Rhonda.

"What thoughtful, thorough girls you are."

"Do you know where we can buy a bouquet with these flowers?"

"I do. Let me make sure I've got them all." She read back the list she'd made as Zoe had been talking.

"That's all of them," Zoe said.

"Let me do some checking around," Rhonda said. "What about other flowers? Is there somewhere in your apartment, Zoe, where it would be nice to have flowers?"

"We have a big window in our living room with a deep windowsill. There are plants in there now, but I could move them for the wedding."

"Excellent. I'll arrange for a bridal bouquet and a big arrangement of the same flowers for the windowsill."

"Will twenty-five dollars pay for both of them?" Diedre asked. "That's how much money we have."

"Don't worry about money," Rhonda said. "I'm happy to contribute these. I'll get to the party by quarter to four—before the other guests arrive. We can put the arrangement in the windowsill."

"And we'll put the bouquet in Zoe's room," Diedre said. "That's where we're going to take Stephanie before you and Dhruv go to the window to announce the wedding."

"What a good idea, girls. I'm so impressed with you."

"Thank you for helping," they said in unison.

"If you need anything else—anything at all—just call me."

Zoe sucked in a breath. "There's one more thing."

"Like I said—anything."

"Can you make sure Dhruv gets a haircut?"

Rhonda guffawed. "I'm not sure, but I'll certainly try. I can't wait to meet the two of you."

"My gramma's calling us," Diedre said as she heard Sylvia's voice coming up the stairs. "We'd better go."

"See you soon, girls. I'm so happy you called."

CHAPTER 48

og shrouded my grassy rest area. I tilted my nose to the air and sniffed, my nostrils flaring. Rain wouldn't be far behind. I liked rain. It ran off my fur as if I was wearing a rain slicker. Licking the moisture off my muzzle was like having my water bowl delivered to me.

Emily, however, did not like rain. Or fog. She stood next to me, her arms circling herself as she pulled her jacket close around herself.

I made short work of my business so we could go back inside. We were up unusually early for a Saturday morning. Especially since we'd stayed up late the night before cleaning our apartment. We usually did that on Saturday mornings, but Emily, Zoe, and Martha had launched into the task with a vengeance as soon as we got home from work. Something big was going down today. I didn't know what, but I could tell by the energy in the room that something was about to happen.

We returned to our apartment to find Martha making coffee. "Here," she said, filling a mug and placing it on the counter. "You can have the first cup."

"Thanks, Mom." Emily hung my working harness on its hook by the door. She went to the pantry and scooped kibble into my bowl. She placed the bowl on the floor in the usual spot, then she slid her hand across the counter until she found her cup.

I was pleased that feeding me was more important than her first cup of coffee. My Emily was the best.

"Is Zoe up yet?" Emily asked.

"I don't think so," Martha said. "I didn't open her door because I was afraid I'd wake her, but I haven't heard any sounds from her room."

"Good. At least one of us should sleep in."

Martha helped herself to a cup of coffee and leaned her back against the counter, bringing the steaming cup to her lips and blowing across the scalding liquid. "It's always hard to relax when you're hosting a party. Let's go over our to-do list."

"Good idea. There really isn't much to do until three, when the Mexican food I ordered arrives."

"Right. We'll keep the trays of beans, rice, enchiladas, and mini burritos warm in the oven," Martha said.

"Yep. We can set out plates, napkins, and silverware as soon as we've cleaned up from breakfast," Emily said. "We'll need bowls for chips and salsa—and for the Crunchy Cheetos."

"Why in the world are you serving Crunchy Cheetos with Mexican food?" Martha asked.

"They're Dhruv's favorite. I figure that since he's going to all the trouble to arrange a surprise birthday party for Stephanie, we ought to have something he really likes, too."

"That's nice. I'm thrilled that he and Stephanie found each other. They're both such dear people—I want them to be happy." Martha took a tentative sip of her coffee. "I wonder if they'll ever get married."

"They're perfect together, I agree," Emily said. "But let's not put the cart before the horse."

"Okay. I just can't help but hope. Anyway—what time will Dhruv be here with the cake?"

"He's going to drop off six extra chairs at nine and then get his hair cut. He'll pick up the cake on his way home."

"We're not going anywhere, so that works."

"I hope he gets it here before it starts to rain. They're predicting storms," Emily said.

"Why don't I make pancakes? They're Zoe's favorite." Martha set her mug on the counter and began gathering ingredients. "And yours, too."

"I'd love that. You spoil us, Mom. What can I do to help?"

"I've got this. Why don't you grab your shower?"

Emily headed toward her bedroom.

I passed by Zoe's door on the way to my bed. A sound behind the door caught my attention and I stopped. Martha had not been correct.

Zoe was awake—and talking to someone softly on the phone.

I listened. I could only hear her side of the conversation and didn't understand all the words. "Wedding" and "surprise" were uttered over and over. Zoe's excited undertone was unmistakable.

Whatever was going on later today, it had to involve birthdays and weddings and surprises. That was as far as I could take it.

One thing was certain: we were going to have a big afternoon. I continued on to my bed. The only thing I could do to help was rest up, so I'd be ready when Emily needed me.

CHAPTER 49

"*I*'ll get it!" Zoe leapt from the sofa and dashed to the door.

Dhruv stood in the hallway, balancing a tall, square, pink bakery box.

"Is that Dhruv, with the cake?" Emily called from the kitchen.

"It's me," he replied.

"There's a spot for the cake at the end of the island," Emily said. "Zoe can show you."

Dhruv followed Zoe to the kitchen island.

"How does it look?" Emily asked. "Did they get the colors right?"

Zoe and Dhruv exchanged glances.

"Yes. It's exactly what you ordered."

"You can take it out of the box," Emily said.

"Why don't we leave it until we're ready to serve it?"

Martha suggested. "There's a fly in here and I can't seem to get rid of it."

"Good thinking," Dhruv said. "We don't want a fly on her cake."

"Do you need help with anything else?" Zoe asked.

"No."

"I'll help, anyway," Zoe said, following Dhruv into the hallway. "I want to go upstairs to see how Stephanie's doing," she said in a stage whisper.

"She's fine."

"You saw her?"

"No! That's bad luck. We've been texting."

"Can I see her?"

"I'm sure she'd like that. I'll walk you up."

"I can go on my own," Zoe said, indignation coloring her voice.

"Emily wouldn't like it. Come on," he said. "We'll take the stairs."

His long legs took the steps two at a time.

Zoe scrambled to keep up. She knocked on the door and announced her presence.

Dhruv waited at the far end of the hall, his back turned to them, until he heard Stephanie's door open and shut again.

"I'm glad you're here," Stephanie said, tightening the sash on her bathrobe. "I can't reach to pull the zipper all the way to the top."

"I'll do it!" Zoe cried. "That's what wedding planners do."

Stephanie smiled in her direction.

"Your hair looks so pretty!" Zoe exclaimed.

"Does it? Is this fancy clip all right?"

"It's perfect. You have bride hair."

"What's Dhruv doing?"

"He just brought the cake over."

"Are you all set?"

"We are, now. We thought Dhruv would bring the cake over this morning. People are supposed to be there in half an hour. We were getting worried."

"He didn't want Martha to see it was a wedding cake, so he brought it over last minute."

"You don't need to worry about that." Zoe told her about the fly.

"I'd better get my dress on." She led Zoe into her bedroom. Her dress was hanging from a hook on the back of her door. She removed her robe and stepped into the dress, reaching around to pull the zipper as high as she could.

Zoe stood behind her and carefully pulled it the rest of the way.

Stephanie tugged at the neckline and ran her hands down the skirt, smoothing folds and patting the pearl embellishments.

Zoe sucked in a breath. "Oh, Stephanie," she whispered. "You're the most beautiful bride ever. Even more than Gina."

Stephanie flushed. "Would you hand me my pink cardigan? It's on the bed."

Zoe handed it to her, and Stephanie slipped her arms into it.

"I'm going to have this on when we arrive, so people don't think I'm wearing a wedding dress." She buttoned the cardigan down the front. It covered the entire bodice of the dress, including all the pearls.

"It looks like you're wearing a pink sweater and a fancy white skirt," Zoe said. "For your birthday."

"Exactly."

"People will yell 'surprise' when you and Dhruv get there. As soon as everyone's said hello, you'll say you have to go to the bathroom, but you'll go to my room," Zoe said. "I'll get your parents and take them to my room."

"That's the plan. I'll take off my sweater. Rhonda will get Dhruv and everyone into the living room."

"And your parents will walk you down the aisle. I'll open my door when we're ready for you."

"I think we've thought of everything," Stephanie said. She took a deep breath. "I can't believe this is actually happening. Dhruv and I are so grateful to you and Emily for my party— and we'll never forget how helpful you and Diedre have been. We couldn't have done it without you."

Zoe circled her arms around Stephanie's waist for a quick hug, then released her. "I'd better get going. Dhruv's waiting for me in the hall."

"See you very soon," Stephanie said, her voice cracking with emotion.

Zoe stood at the door to their apartment, buzzing people into the lobby and opening the door. Grant and Diedre were the first guests to arrive.

Diedre raised her eyebrows at Zoe as she stepped inside.

Zoe gave her a quick thumbs-up sign in response.

Grant found Emily in the kitchen where she and Martha were placing cans of soda and bottles of water into a chrome beverage bucket filled with ice. He bent and they shared a peck of a kiss.

"Hi, Martha," he said, turning to her. "Where can I put this?" He held up a small white gift bag filled with deep pink tissue paper.

"We thought we'd put gifts on the windowsill in the living room," Martha said as Zoe and Diedre joined them in the kitchen.

"No!" Zoe cried. "No," she said more calmly. "We'll put them on the table to the left of the door."

"When did we decide that?" Emily asked.

"Just now. Diedre and I think it's better. The window sill won't be big enough." She reached for the gift bag. "I'll put it there for you."

"Thank you."

Zoe and Diedre headed off with Grant's gift.

"That was nice of you to get her something," Emily said.

"We wouldn't come to a birthday party without a present. Diedre picked it out. It's perfume."

"What a thoughtful gift. She'll love it," Martha chimed in. "I've noticed that she likes to wear scent."

The doorbell rang.

"We'll get the door for all the guests," Zoe yelled as she opened the door to Rhonda, right on time.

"Is the coast clear?" Rhonda asked softly.

Zoe glanced over her shoulder to confirm that the adults remained in the kitchen. "Yeah. Where are the flowers?"

Rhonda stepped back into the hallway and pointed to the floor to the right of the door. "I stashed them here in case you weren't the one to answer the door. These might be a dead giveaway." She picked up a bridal bouquet fashioned of creamy gardenias, pink hyacinths, and lily of the valley and pressed it into Diedre's outstretched arms.

"Wow," Diedre said, inhaling deeply. "These smell amazing." She turned and rushed to hide them in Zoe's bedroom.

Zoe lifted the large, lush arrangement of the same flowers and carried it to the windowsill in the living room.

Rhonda followed and repositioned the few stems that had become dislodged on the journey from the florist.

They both stood back and admired the scene in front of them. The blinds were open. The rain had stopped and diffuse late afternoon sunshine outlined the delicate blooms that filled the lower half of the window. A deep, cloudless aquamarine sky was visible behind the flowers. The staging was worthy of a photo shoot. Rhonda and Zoe looked at each other and nodded.

"I'm Rhonda, by the way." She held her hand out to Zoe. "I feel like I already know you, from all the wonderful things Emily has told me about you."

They shook hands. Zoe's cheeks flushed and a shy smile planted itself on her lips.

"I think I should stand right here, facing the other end of the room." Rhonda spun around and placed the windowsill behind her back. "Dhruv will be on my left." She motioned with her hand. "Here. You said Stephanie's parents will both walk her down the aisle?"

Zoe nodded.

Rhonda looked at the room in front of her. "This will work well." Pointing to two chairs in the middle of the room, she said, "Let's move those two back a bit. That'll give enough room for them to walk across the room to Dhruv and me."

Zoe nodded, and they moved the chairs.

Diedre joined them.

"You're the other co-conspirator," Rhonda whispered.

Diedre nodded enthusiastically.

"Let's make sure we're all on the same page."

Both girls turned serious eyes to hers.

"As soon as Stephanie and Biscuit go into Zoe's room, Zoe will get Stephanie's parents to follow them," Rhonda said.

Diedre and Zoe nodded.

"I imagine Stephanie and her parents will get emotional when she tells them what's about to happen. They may need a moment to gather themselves. When they're ready, Zoe will tell Diedre. Diedre will then find me. I'll come and stand here." She pointed to her feet. "Dhruv will be with his parents. I'll get everyone's attention and ask them to take a seat in the living room." She looked around herself. "Can you get me a glass and a knife?"

Zoe furrowed her brows. "Why?"

"I'll strike the glass with the knife. That'll make everyone stop talking."

"Like at Gina's wedding reception," Diedre said, clasping her hands together and looking at Zoe's puzzled expression. "They did that right before the toasts."

Zoe swung her head back. "Yep."

"I'll explain that we're all gathered together to celebrate not just Stephanie's birthday, but her and Dhruv's wedding. That'll get everyone talking. Dhruv will usher his parents to these chairs." Rhonda pointed to her left.

"Once his parents are seated and Dhruv's standing with you," Diedre said to Rhonda, "I'll knock on Zoe's door to tell Stephanie and her parents it's time to come out."

"As soon as Stephanie and her parents leave my room, we'll put the veil on Biscuit," Zoe said.

"Stephanie's parents will sit in these chairs after she's joined Dhruv and me." Rhonda touched the chairs.

"I'll take Biscuit to Emily," Zoe said.

"And Dhruv will ask Emily and Biscuit to join them."

"When Emily and Biscuit are with Stephanie and Dhruv, I'll begin the ceremony." Rhonda put her arms around the two girls and hugged them. "You've both done an excellent job helping Dhruv plan his wedding. He talks about the two of you all the time." Her voice grew thick with emotion. "I've worked with him for years and I couldn't be happier for him. I'm honored and thrilled to be officiating."

"Who was at the door, honey?" Emily's voice came closer as she exited the kitchen.

"It's me, Emily," Rhonda said. "I wrote the time down wrong in my calendar and got here a bit too early." She crossed the living room to intercept Emily. "Do you need help with anything?"

"No. We're all set. Guests should be here any minute now."

As if on cue, the bell rang.

Zoe and Diedre raced to the door and welcomed Dhruv's parents and his uncle. Next to arrive were Stephanie's parents. The final guest was Doug Roberts.

Grant stationed himself in the kitchen pouring drinks that the girls ferried out to guests.

Emily hugged Stephanie's mother and father and introduced them to Dhruv's parents and uncle. They greeted each other enthusiastically, their shared joy that Stephanie and Dhruv had found each other radiating from each of them.

Doug drew Martha to one side. "You girls know how to throw a party. Everything looks great."

"Thank you. I'm proud of Emily. She's a terrific hostess."

"I'll bet she's learned that from you."

Martha flushed. "I enjoy having people over."

"The food smells wonderful. So do those flowers in the living room. That was a nice touch."

"They're gorgeous, aren't they? I have to admit—we didn't think of them. Someone else must have brought them." She gazed at the flowers. "They almost look like they should be on an altar, or something."

Emily clapped her hands over her head. The chatter in the room stopped. "Dhruv just texted. They're on their way."

Everyone turned to face the door and remained silent.

The bell rang.

Emily opened the door wide and moved back.

Dhruv led Stephanie over the threshold, Biscuit at her side.

The assembled guests erupted in a chorus of, "SURPRISE!"

Stephanie brought her hand to her heart and clutched her sweater.

"HAPPY BIRTHDAY," yelled the group.

Stephanie replaced the shocked look on her face with a smile.

Her mother was the first to reach her, planting a kiss on her cheek.

Stephanie and Dhruv began circulating with the guests.

Zoe and Diedre took Biscuit to Zoe's room.

"You ready?" Diedre asked Zoe.

Zoe nodded.

The two girls threw their arms around each other.

"This is so much fun," Zoe whispered in Diedre's ear.

"Should be any minute now," Diedre whispered back.

They stepped apart, nodded at each other, and got themselves into position.

CHAPTER 50

Zoe ushered Stephanie's parents into her bedroom and quickly closed the door behind them.

Stephanie had removed her pink cardigan and stood with her back to the door, holding her wedding bouquet in front of her. She turned to them as the door clicked shut.

Stephanie's father gasped.

"Stephanie," her mother began. "You look like…"

"A bride?" Stephanie interjected. "That's because I am. Dhruv and I are getting married. *Here. Now.*"

Her mother brought her hand to her heart. "Oh, honey," she said, her voice wavering.

"We wanted our parents to be with us, but we didn't want a big wedding." She stepped toward them. "I hope you understand, and that you're not hurt. Or disappointed."

Her mother closed the gap between them. "Of course we're not. I'm… we're… just surprised, is all."

Stephanie reached out her free hand, and her father took it in his.

"We want whatever you want, honey," he said, closing his palm over the top of her hand.

"Dhruv and I are so happy together. We've both known— from the very beginning—that we wanted to spend the rest of our lives together. I didn't think you'd care if we went to the courthouse, but Dhruv felt his parents might have a hard time with that. He couldn't stand the idea of the huge, days-long wedding celebrations that are typical in his culture." She shook her head. "I wouldn't have wanted that, either. We decided this was the best way. For us."

A tear coursed down her mother's cheek.

Zoe handed her a tissue from the box on her bedside table.

"Will you both walk me down the aisle?"

"Of course," her father croaked.

"Can I tell Diedre you're ready?" Zoe asked.

"Wait! One minute." Her mother spun to Zoe. "Would you get our gift to Stephanie and bring it here? It's in a long, thin box wrapped in yellow paper and tied with a green ribbon."

"Sure." Zoe slipped out the door.

Stephanie's mother cupped her daughter's chin in her hand. "It's your grandmother's pearls. She gave them to me before she died and asked that we give them to you on your thirty-fifth birthday. You can wear them to get married."

"Oh, Mom. That's wonderful. I didn't have anything old." Stephanie blinked rapidly. "Darn it," she said, sniffling loudly. "I don't want to cry and mess up my makeup."

Stephanie's mother plucked another tissue from the box. "Your grandmother would be thrilled that you're wearing her pearls at your wedding." She dabbed at her daughter's eyes and patted the dampness from her cheeks. "There. Every hair's in place and you haven't got a smudge anywhere."

The door opened a crack, and Zoe slid back into the room. She handed the box to Stephanie.

Stephanie carefully unwrapped the heirloom gift.

Her mother secured the strand of pearls around Stephanie's neck and took a step back. "There. They mirror the pearls on your dress. Just what you needed. Your dress is so beautiful, honey. You look perfect."

"The one thing I regret is that we didn't get to go wedding dress shopping together, Mom," Stephanie said softly.

"Don't give that a second thought." Her mother's voice was thick with emotion. "It wouldn't have been fair for one set of parents to know and not the other. You did the right thing by not telling us."

"You've always been the best, Mom." Stephanie ran her fingers over the smooth, cool spheres. "I can feel Grandma with me."

"I can, too," her mother said in a breathy whisper.

Stephanie took her father's elbow and linked arms with her mother, holding her bouquet in front of her. "We're ready," she said to Zoe. "I'm ready to marry Dhruv."

～

RHONDA REMOVED A SMALL, leather-bound notebook from her purse. She checked to make sure that the bookmark was placed in the correct page for her notes on the upcoming ceremony. She picked up the glass and knife from behind the flowers and positioned herself in front of the window. The sun lit the arrangement like a spotlight. She tapped on the glass and the other guests, congregating at the far end of the room, turned to face her.

Dhruv, tall and elegant in his navy blue raw silk sherwani, towered over the others.

Rhonda and Dhruv nodded at each other. He moved to stand behind his parents.

"Thank you for your attention," Rhonda said. "We've already had one surprise this afternoon. I hope you're ready for another."

All conversation ceased, and everyone's eyes were fixed on her.

"This isn't only Stephanie's birthday. It's also Dhruv and Stephanie's wedding. It'll be my honor to perform the ceremony."

A murmur of surprise rippled through the group. Dhruv's parents whipped their heads around to stare at him.

Dhruv wordlessly nodded his agreement with Rhonda's proclamation.

His parents stood, mouths agape, while everyone else held their breath, waiting for their reaction.

Dhruv's mother elevated her tiny frame as high as her tiptoes would take her and seized his shoulders, drawing Dhruv into a fierce hug.

His father circled them both with his arms and the three of them stood in a group hug. He finally pulled back and unhooked the thick gold chain that Dhruv had never seen his father without. He placed it around Dhruv's neck and fastened the clasp.

"Dad—no," Dhruv protested, reaching up to remove it.

His father placed his hand over Dhruv's to stop him. "I received this from my father when I married your mother. I always intended it to be yours on your wedding day."

Dhruv swallowed hard as his father clapped him on the back. "Thank you," he whispered, then steered his parents to the chairs on Rhonda's left before taking his place next to her.

"Would everyone please take a seat?" Rhonda gestured to the two chairs on her right. "These are reserved for Stephanie's parents."

Everyone quickly sat.

Martha fished in the pocket of her slacks for a tissue.

Doug patted her knee.

Martha smiled up at him. "I always cry at weddings," she said.

"I remember that."

Diedre knocked on Zoe's bedroom door, then opened it wide.

Stephanie and her parents stepped into the hallway and began their trek to the living room.

Zoe and Diedre darted into Zoe's bedroom. They snatched the bridal veil they'd fashioned from its hiding spot in Zoe's closet and placed it on Biscuit's head.

Everyone swiveled to see the bride and her parents as they made their way slowly across the living room, their steps in unison.

Dhruv's parents turned back to look at their son as he watched his bride walk to him.

Dhruv only had eyes for Stephanie. His smile shone like a beacon.

Stephanie's parents placed her on Rhonda's right side. Her father shook Dhruv's hand, and both of her parents sank into the vacant chairs that Rhonda pointed to.

Rhonda nodded at Dhruv.

He addressed the group. "Stephanie and I would like Emily and Biscuit to join us," he said. "You've both been such important parts of our lives. We want you to stand with us."

Emily spun to Grant, who sat next to her at the back of the room.

He helped her to her feet.

"Emily," Zoe said in a stage whisper.

Emily turned toward her, and Zoe handed her Biscuit's harness. "Find Stephanie," Emily said.

Biscuit guided Emily the short distance to her beloved handler.

The guests smiled and pointed to Biscuit's veil.

Stephanie pressed her bouquet into Emily's hands. She reached down to pat Biscuit and touched the scratchy tulle. Stephanie felt the netting with her hand and a huge smile flooded her face when she realized Biscuit was wearing a bridal veil.

Emily drew Dhruv into a fierce hug. "I'm so thankful that

you and Stephanie found each other. You—of all people—deserve a lifetime of happiness, Dhruv," she whispered in his ear before releasing him.

Dhruv placed Emily next to him and Biscuit stood with Stephanie.

Rhonda dabbed at her own eyes, then cleared her throat, and uttered the time-honored words, "Dearly Beloved, we are gathered here today…"

She introduced herself and said, "One of my favorite passages from literature is this observation about love, written decades ago by Charlotte Bronte in Jane Eyre. I think it holds true today:

"I have for the first time found what I can truly love—I have found you. You are my sympathy—my better self—my good angel—I am bound to you with a strong attachment. I think you good, gifted, lovely; a fervent, a solemn passion is conceived in my heart; it leans to you, draws you to my centre and spring of life, wraps my existence about you—and, kindling in pure, powerful flame, fuses you and me in one."

She closed her notebook when she finished the reading. "It's now time for the couple to make their solemn vows to each other. Please face each other and take hands."

Dhruv and Stephanie did as instructed.

"Dhruv," Rhonda prompted.

Dhruv held Stephanie's hands with a palpable gentleness. He looked down at her upturned face and breathed deeply. The others in the room, in this moment, did not exist to him.

"Stephanie. When I met you, I knew one thing for sure. My prayers had been answered. I'd been asking for my special person—my soul mate—for years. At times, I'd become discouraged—almost given up—and then I met you and all doubt evaporated. Thank you for embracing the parts of me that make me who I am. Thank you for celebrating all that I am and looking with grace at all that I am not."

Both mothers wept.

Dhruv pulled a rumpled piece of paper from his pocket and read. "I promise to be faithful and supportive through all the seasons of our life—whether they are easy or hard—in plenty and in want, in sickness and in health, in failure and triumph. I will never let you forget how talented, loving, capable, and beautiful you are. I will talk when you need words and be quiet when you need silence. I will always be a safe place for your dreams and your fears. We will face everything together. I give you my hand and my heart as a sanctuary of warmth and peace as we join our lives today."

By the time he had finished, everyone in the room was sniffling and swiping at tears.

Stephanie squeezed Dhruv's hands, then began. "My darling Dhruv. I realized the moment I met you that you were 'the one.' You are an incredibly brilliant man, but as big as your brain is—your heart is bigger. Your empathy and kindness know no bounds. Your tenacity has changed lives."

Emily gulped and nodded in agreement.

"I admire all the good that you quietly bring to this world —without ever looking for recognition or thanks. You are blessed with the rare heart of a servant and you enrich the life of every person you come into contact with. I will spend the rest of my days celebrating your spirit and accomplishments. I will work to inspire you and will remind you of your beauty and strength. I pledge my love and devotion—always—and will honor you all the days of my life."

Rhonda took a shuddering breath and cleared her throat before leading them through the exchange of rings. When they were done, she continued, "By the power vested in me, I now pronounce you husband and wife. You may now kiss the bride."

Dhruv swept Stephanie into his arms and they clung to each other, kissing, their bodies swaying slightly.

Biscuit sneezed loudly, breaking the spell.

Everyone laughed.

Stephanie grasped Biscuit's harness, and the newlyweds turned to the assembled group, who were now on their feet clapping and surging forward to congratulate the couple.

CHAPTER 51

I lifted my head from my paws. People were moving toward the kitchen. I glanced over at Biscuit, who still wore that scratchy thing on her head. Everyone had exclaimed over it and seemed to think it was so funny. They'd been congratulating Zoe and Diedre about it—telling them how clever they were. I didn't agree—it looked ridiculous. I'd been keeping a low profile—I didn't want anyone to get the idea that I needed one of those things.

After all the crying and kissing in the living room, people had come into the kitchen to help themselves to the food Emily had set out on the island. I'd raised up on my front legs, alert to any morsels that might have dropped off of a plate or been knocked off the counter. Cleaning up spills was the least I could do. Sadly, there hadn't been any. Sabrina was on high alert, too. We'd do a thorough sweep of the living room later, after everyone left. Surely we'd find some scraps then.

Everyone had returned to the kitchen. Martha and Doug had removed the food from the counter—if I had to guess, I'd say it had been Mexican cuisine—and placed a cake in the middle of the island.

Dhruv led Stephanie to the cake and, hands clasped together, they cut the first slice. I blinked hard at what came next. Dhruv picked up a piece of cake—with his fingers—and placed it in Stephanie's mouth. No fork or anything.

She then did the same for him, but I thought the piece she picked up was far too large for a human mouth. I would have been fine with it, of course, but not Dhruv. She also didn't get it into his mouth as neatly as he had done with hers. Biscuit and I exchanged glances, and I knew she was thinking the same thing I was. Stephanie couldn't see Dhruv's mouth and shouldn't be criticized for making such a mess of it. It seems the humans agreed. Everyone laughed and clapped as Dhruv wiped frosting from his face with a napkin.

I settled down on my bed next to Biscuit and Sabrina. You'd have thought we would have been crowded on this bed, what with two of us being the size we were, but we all enjoyed curling up together. We were part of a pack again.

I was almost asleep when whistles and clapping brought me back to full consciousness. I wandered into the living room to learn what all the fuss was about.

Stephanie stood in front of the window with her back to

the room. Emily, Zoe, Diedre, and Martha stood in a ring around her.

"Okay, single ladies," Stephanie said.

Zoe and Diedre giggled.

"Are you ready?" She swung her arms over her head, her bouquet in her hands. When her hands had crested the top of the arc and started down the other side, she released the bouquet.

The flowers sailed through the air on a trajectory between Diedre and Emily.

Diedre bumped Emily with her hip, sending her firmly into the path of the bouquet.

The flowers grazed her chin and slid down the front of her blouse, but Emily grasped them before they slid to the floor.

The group cheered and whistled. "You're the next one to get married," someone called.

Zoe and Diedre grinned at each other behind Emily's back.

"Time for the garter," Diedre announced.

"I don't have one," Stephanie said.

"Yes, you do," the girls said in unison. "We made you one."

Diedre fished the blue hair-scrunchy-turned-garter out of her pocket and handed it to Stephanie.

"Okay, gentlemen. I think that means Grant, Doug, and Dhruv's uncle need to line up behind me," Stephanie said, turning her back on them.

She repeated her motions and sent the scrunchy flying.

All three men reached for it.

Grant sprang into the air and snatched it away from the others.

The group erupted again.

"Grant got it," Zoe cried, going to Emily. "You caught the bouquet and Grant caught the garter at Gina's wedding, and now this one. That means you should get married."

Emily drew Zoe to her and smoothed Zoe's hair away from her forehead. "There wasn't much competition for the garter," she said.

"Yes, there was. All the men were trying to get it. Grant jumped and made sure he caught it." Her voice was full of hope. She tilted her chin to look at Emily. "You want this, too, don't you? I can tell."

Emily bent and pressed a kiss into Zoe's hair. "Maybe I do. Time will tell. Grant and I need to get to know each other better, and we need to consider how you and Diedre would feel about it."

"We want to be sisters," Zoe said.

"We'll talk about this later," Emily said. "It sounds like Stephanie and Dhruv are saying goodbye to their parents. They must be getting ready to leave."

People began congregating at the door, commenting on what a moving wedding it had been and how glad they were to have been there.

Diedre removed the veil from Biscuit and Stephanie put Biscuit into her working harness.

I decided to get out of everyone's way and headed back to my bed. A familiar hand emanating from a navy blue sherwani intercepted me in the kitchen.

"You haven't gotten a single snack today, have you, boy?" Dhruv rubbed my ears in that wonderful way of his and looked around himself nervously.

I wagged my tail.

Dhruv reached up and plucked a handful of Crunchy Cheetos from a bowl on the island. He cupped them in the palm of his hand, which he held out to me.

Who was I to say no to a groom on his wedding day? Dhruv and I shared a passion for Crunchy Cheetos. I downed *my* favorite food in one bite and licked every crumb of the orange, cheesy powder from his fingers. There'd be no telltale residue on his fancy wedding clothes.

He patted the top of my head one more time, then went to join his bride.

I continued to my bed, with a heart full of happiness over the events of the day and the taste of Crunchy Cheetos on my lips.

THE END

THANK YOU FOR READING

If you enjoyed *Over Every Hurdle*, I'd be grateful if you wrote a review.

Just a few lines on Amazon or Goodreads would be great. Reviews are the best gift an author can receive. They encourage us when they're good, help us improve our next book when they're not, and help other readers make informed choices when purchasing books. Goodreads reviews help readers find new books. Reviews on Amazon keep the Amazon algorithms humming and are the most helpful aide in selling books! Thank you.

To post a review on Amazon:

1. Go to the product detail page for *Over Every Hurdle* on Amazon.com.

2. Click "Write a customer review" in the Customer Reviews section.

3. Write your review and click Submit.

In gratitude,
Barbara Hinske

ACKNOWLEDGMENTS

I'm blessed with the wisdom and support of many kind and generous people. I want to thank the most supportive and delightful group of champions an author could hope for:

Steve Pawlowski for starting me on this most gratifying path;

My insightful and supportive assistant Lisa Coleman who keeps all the plates spinning;

My life coach Mat Boggs for your wisdom and guidance;

My kind and generous legal team, Kenneth Kleinberg, Esq., and Michael McCarthy—thank you for believing in my vision;

The professional "dream team" of my editors Linden Gross, Kelly Byrd, and proofreader Dana Lee;

Elizabeth Mackey for a beautiful cover.

RECURRING CHARACTERS

Connor Harrington III: highly successful sales executive; Emily's ex-husband.

Dhruv: genius senior programmer on Emily's team; husband of Stephanie; dogs are **Sugar** (golden retriever) and **Rocco** (dachshund).

Gerald: Executive Vice President at Connor's employer.

Howard Kent: Executive Vice President of Systems and Programming at Emily's employer; a champion of Emily.

Irene: Zoe's grandmother.

JOHNSON

Craig Johnson: twin brother of Grant; married to Gina Roberts; veterinarian.

Diedre Johnson: daughter of Grant.

Grant Johnson: twin brother of Craig; love interest of Emily; widowed father of Diedre; architect.

Sylvia Johnson: widowed mother of Craig and Grant; grandmother of Diedre.

Julie Ross: counselor at the Foundation for the Blind; her guide dog is **Golda**.

Karen: works at makeup counter at Nordstrom.

Kari: senior programmer on the cyber security team at Emily's employer in Denver office.

Katie and John: Garth's puppy raisers; their children are **Alex** and **Abby**; their cat is **Liloh**.

MAIN

Emily Main: department head of a top-notch programming team at a technology giant; lost her eyesight when her retinas detached in a riding accident on her honeymoon; divorced from Connor; daughter of Martha; Zoe is her ward; love interest of Grant; Gina is her lifelong best friend: **Garth** (black lab) is her guide dog.

Martha Main: widowed mother of Emily.

Michael Ward: supervisor in Emily's team of programmers.

Rhonda: programmer in Emily's team.

ROBERTS

Doug Roberts: uncle of Gina; love interest of Martha.

Gina Roberts: lifelong best friend of Emily; married to Craig; parents are Hilary and Charles.

Hilary and Charles Roberts: Gina's parents (retired); Gina's mother is a breast cancer survivor.

Roger Foley: Connor's boss and Asia Region Senior Vice President.

Ross Wilcox: director of cyber security team of programmers at Emily's employer in the Denver office.

Scott Dalton: Connor's best friend.

Spencer Chamberlain: orientation and mobility specialist at the Foundation for the Blind.

Stephanie Wolf: close friend and classmate of Emily at the Foundation for the Blind; third grade teacher; wife of Dhruv; guide dog is **Biscuit** (yellow lab).

Zoe: parents killed in a car accident; lives with her grandmother and becomes Emily's ward when her grandmother (Irene) dies, leaving Zoe in Emily's care; dog is **Sabrina** (miniature schnauzer).

PLEASE ENJOY THIS EXCERPT FROM DOWN THE AISLE

"Emily," Zoe called as she pushed open their front door. "Stephanie's sick again. Can you walk me to school?"

Emily slid her laptop into her satchel and zipped it shut. "Of course," she said. "I thought you would have been halfway there by now. You said she was feeling better last night when you were playing Scrabble with her and Dhruv."

"She was. And she was waiting for me this morning, as usual, but when we got to the sidewalk, Stephanie said she wasn't feeling well again. We had to turn around and come back. She kept saying 'sorry.'"

Emily called to Garth, the black lab with the coat as shiny as a seal, and put him into his working harness. "That stomach bug's really taken hold of her. It's miserable to feel nauseated." She lifted her white cane from the entryway table and tucked it under her arm. "Let's go. We'll let Garth walk at top speed and you'll be on time for school."

"Yeah! He loves to zoom along."

"He certainly does."

The threesome hurried down the steps to the sidewalk. Emily commanded Garth to follow Zoe, and they stepped out into the early morning fog, traversing the few blocks to Hillside Elementary and arriving as the first bell sounded.

"I'll come get you after school," Emily said.

"I'm in fifth grade, Em," Zoe whined. "I can walk home by myself."

"You are NOT to do that," Emily replied. "I'll come for you."

"But..."

"We're not having this conversation right now. It's late. You need to get to class and I have to go to work." Emily reached out an arm to the girl who had become her ward when Zoe's grandmother had died almost two years before; the girl she loved like a daughter.

Zoe slid into her embrace for a one-armed hug. "All right."

"Have a good day." Emily resisted the urge to plant a kiss on top of Zoe's dark, curly-haired head. She remembered how self-conscious she had been at Zoe's age.

"You too," Zoe said as her voice trailed off into the sea of children surging past Emily to get into their seats before the second bell rang.

Emily and Garth remained in place until the surrounding chaos subsided.

"Find the gate," Emily commanded, and Garth took her, as he'd been trained, to the iron gate fixed to a brick column emblazoned with the words "Hillside Elementary School."

"Good boy!" she said, rubbing his ears and along his jawline in the way she knew he loved. "Garth—home."

Garth took off at a brisk clip, following the command he knew so well. They had just crossed the last street and stepped onto their block when Emily heard a familiar voice calling her name.

"Emily!" Dhruv called as he sprinted the distance between them. His voice held an unmistakable tone of panic.

"What's happened? Is Stephanie okay?"

"Yes—she's fine. I mean no..." Dhruv stammered. "She's sick, but that's not it."

"What's wrong, then?"

"It's happened."

"What's happened?"

"We've been attacked. The company's been hacked. None of our systems work and the attackers are demanding a two-hundred-million-dollar ransom."

Emily froze and turned toward her tall, lanky employee. "How do you know?"

"Kari texted me to call her."

"And?"

"She told me we've been the subject of a cyberattack and the attackers have demanded this huge ransom. Ross has been trying to call you."

Emily patted the pocket of her jacket. "I must have left my phone at home. Zoe and I ran out the door pretty fast when Stephanie—when Zoe said she needed me to walk her to school."

"I was worried," Dhruv said. "You never go anywhere without your phone. Then I remembered about Zoe, and I figured I'd find you on your way home."

"Good thinking. Have you tried to log in this morning?"

"I left my laptop at the office on Friday. I wanted to focus on Stephanie since she wasn't feeling well."

"Let's go check mine," Emily said. She and Garth set off behind Dhruv, sprinting to keep up with his long-legged strides.

"Kari said no one in the company can get logged into the company's intranet." Dhruv turned off the sidewalk and ran up the steps to the apartment building where they both occupied spacious, older units on the first floor.

Garth took Emily to her apartment.

Emily opened the door and removed Garth's guide dog harness in one practiced motion, hanging it on its designated hook. She walked the familiar path to the kitchen island, where she'd left her satchel with her laptop.

Dhruv closed the door behind them.

Emily tugged her laptop from her satchel and spoke her password into her speech recognition software program. The laptop came to life. Her attempt to log into her company's intranet failed.

Dhruv hovered over her shoulder.

"Well?" Emily asked.

"Nothing. It's a completely blank screen."

"Oh, no!" Emily felt along the countertop until she found her phone. She tapped at the screen and listened as the screen reader told her she had eight missed calls—five from Kari; two from Ross Wilcox, head of the cybersecurity division of the company and Kari's boss; and one from Howard Kent, executive vice president of Systems and Programming at her company. Only Howard had left a message. Emily tapped the screen to listen to Howard's message.

"Emily. Howard Kent here. You'll know by now about the cybersecurity breach. I need you and Dhruv on a flight to Denver ASAP. One of the corporate jets is waiting for you at San Jose International Airport and a driver will pick you both up from the office in ninety minutes. Text me when you're on your way to the airport. Ross will fill you in while you're in the air. Plan to be in Denver indefinitely."

Dhruv's breath was coming in short bursts. "This is what I tried to warn them about. We knew this would happen."

Emily inhaled deeply, trying to quell the panic she felt. She was well aware of the devastating effects of recent ransomware attacks on major businesses. Several National Health Service systems in England and Scotland had been targets in 2017, causing catastrophic disruptions to patient care and a £92-million loss. Then in September 2020, the Universal Health Services (UHS) were infected with a strain of malware called Ryuk. UHS decided not to pay the ransom and worked with outside security experts to regain access to UHS's systems and data. The attack still cost UHS $67 million.

Another hacker crew calling itself the DarkSide used a strain of Evil malware to attack oil pipeline system Colonial Pipeline. Colonial was forced to close its 5,500-mile pipeline on the East Coast until it paid a $4.4-million ransom in Bitcoin. The FBI later recovered some of the ransom. Even if a company paid a ransom, there was no guarantee that the attackers would restore a company's data and systems.

"We don't know exactly what's happened, Dhruv."

"I do..."

Emily put up a hand to stop him. "We'll have plenty of time to talk on the plane. Right now, I have to call my mom to ask her if she can come into the city to stay with Zoe. And I need to pack for me and for Garth." She raked her fingers through her hair. "Can you make this trip?"

"Yes."

"Go get packed and come back here. We'll take a rideshare to the office. Howard's voicemail came in twenty minutes ago, so we need to be on our way to the office in under thirty minutes."

"It won't take me long to pack. We can put Garth's food in my carry-on bag."

"That'll be really helpful. Make sure you have your ID with you. We may not be flying home on the company plane. Bring whatever you'll need for a commercial flight."

Dhruv was already at the door.

"And Dhruv," Emily called to him. "We don't know what is public knowledge at this point, so don't tell Stephanie why we're going."

"I won't," he assured her, "but she'll guess." He closed the door behind him.

Emily nodded in agreement with this prediction. Dhruv had been warning of a cyberattack on the company ever since their ill-fated interactions with the cybersecurity division several months before. She placed the call to her mother, Martha Main, and tried to calm her racing thoughts while she waited for her to answer.

Down the Aisle

ABOUT THE AUTHOR

USA Today Bestselling Author BARBARA HINSKE is an attorney and novelist. She's authored the Guiding Emily series, the mystery thriller collection "Who's There?", the Paws & Pastries series, two novellas in The Wishing Tree series, and the beloved *Rosemont Series*. Her novella *The Christmas Club* was made into a Hallmark Channel movie of the same name in 2019.

She is extremely grateful to her readers! She inherited the writing gene from her father who wrote mysteries when he retired and told her a story every night of her childhood. She and her husband share their own Rosemont with two adorable and spoiled dogs. The old house keeps her husband busy with repair projects and her happily decorating, entertaining, and gardening. She also spends a lot of time baking and—as a result—dieting.

ALSO BY BARBARA HINSKE

Available at Amazon in Print, Audio, and for Kindle

The Rosemont Series

Coming to Rosemont

Weaving the Strands

Uncovering Secrets

Drawing Close

Bringing Them Home

Shelving Doubts

Restoring What Was Lost

No Matter How Far

When Dreams There Be

Novellas

The Night Train

The Christmas Club (adapted

for The Hallmark Channel, 2019)

Paws & Pastries

Sweets & Treats

Snowflakes, Cupcakes & Kittens (coming 2023)

Workout Wishes & Valentine Kisses

Wishes of Home

Novels in the Guiding Emily Series

Guiding Emily

The Unexpected Path

Over Every Hurdle

Down the Aisle

Novels in the "Who's There?!" Collection

Deadly Parcel

Final Circuit

CONNECT WITH BARBARA HINSKE ONLINE

Sign up for her newsletter at **BarbaraHinske.com**
Goodreads.com/BarbaraHinske
Facebook.com/BHinske
Instagram/barbarahinskeauthor
TikTok.com/BarbaraHinske
Pinterest.com/BarbaraHinske
Twitter.com/BarbaraHinske
Search for **Barbara Hinske on YouTube**
bhinske@gmail.com

Made in United States
Orlando, FL
24 December 2023

41650350R00200